D1257928

ANNIE'S ATTIC MYSTERIES ®

Jazzed

Donna Kelly

Annie's ®
AnniesFiction.com

Library of Congress-in-Publication Data
Jazzed / by Donna Kelly
p. cm.
I. Title
                    2012920433

AnniesFiction.com
800-282-6643
Annie's Attic Mysteries®
Series Editors: Ken and Janice Tate
Series Creator: Stenhouse & Associates, Ridgefield, Connecticut

10 11 12 13 14 | Printed in China | 9 8 7 6 5

~Dedication~

This book is dedicated, in respectful memory, to Herman Leonard (1923–2010), considered by many—including the author—to have been "the greatest jazz photographer in the world." Thank you for capturing the soul of jazz on film and sharing it with the world.

~ 1 ~

ingers wrapped around a mug of hot mint tea, Annie
Dawson inhaled the comforting aroma, hands warming
on the ceramic and face tingling as the steam curled under
her nose. Gazing out of the living room bay window, she
watched the wind whip bare lilac bush branches and bend
sugar maple treetops. Beyond the trees, narrow footpath,
and rocky beach, the sea rolled relentlessly toward shore,
the one constant in a world of change.

Her walk on the beach earlier that afternoon had been
glorious—the juxtaposition of icy wind and brilliant sun
offering the hope of coming spring. Winter had been long
and harsh, and now was reluctant to release its grip on
the weather.

She stood almost motionless at the window, sporadically lifting the mug to her lips, and was surprised to see
the postman winding up the walkway with a small package
in his hands.

Placing the empty mug on the doily-topped table below
the window, Annie opened the front door before he had time
to ring the bell.

"Hey, Al," she said, her Southern accent greeting the
native Mainer. "Come in; you must be frozen!"

Stepping inside the door, he held the box out to Annie
after she closed the door against the cold.

"Not more than usual for this time of year. The wind is fierce, but spring is just around the corner. I feel it in my bones," the postman said, reaching for the doorknob.

"I'm glad your bones are better at picking up on weather patterns than mine," Annie said, laughing as she glanced at the rather flat, square package in her hand. She smiled at the return address. It had traveled all the way from Texas—where her daughter, LeeAnn, and family were already basking in beautiful, mild weather—to blustery Stony Point, Maine.

"Stay warm, Al. And thanks for bringing this package from back home right to my front door," she said.

After she had closed the door behind him, Annie ran her fingers across the box and imagined LeeAnn taking care to align the tape just so before pressing it along the cardboard. Even as a mother of rambunctious twins in constant demand of her attention, LeeAnn was still a perfectionist.

Annie lifted her head as an odd noise, sounding like a cross between a cat's meow and a baby's laugh, came from the hallway.

"Boots, we have an unexpected present from LeeAnn!" she told the gray, white-pawed cat, now cocking its head and looking at her with what appeared to be amusement. She carried the package to the nearby couch, plopped down on the dark green cushions, and chuckled as the cat jumped up beside her.

"You're curious too, aren't you?" Annie said, scratching the furry head now resting against her thigh.

Grabbing scissors from her crochet bag nestled on the floor beside the sofa, Annie slit the tape on the box and pulled out its contents—a double CD set of jazz featuring her favorite artists!

On the back was a note written in LeeAnn's neat, but embellished, cursive writing:

Dear Mom,

I'll always remember when I'd walk into the living room and see you and Dad dancing your hearts out to jazz music. Remember when I would "dance" with Dad by standing on his feet? When I found this CD set, I just knew you had to have it!

Keep dancing, Mom ...
I love you,
LeeAnn

Smiling at the memory of a young LeeAnn dancing with her father, Annie's eyes misted. The twins were only four years old when Wayne died unexpectedly from a heart attack. John and Joanna would never know the joy of dancing with their grandfather.

She moved Boots, who blinked her green eyes in displeasure, with one hand and rose with the CD case in the other. Annie's grandmother, Elizabeth Holden, had purchased a small, portable CD player in an attempt to keep up with the modern world. Not quite able to let go of the past, she kept it perched on top of the huge, old, walnut-encased record player.

Annie chuckled at her own inability to let go of the old wooden dinosaur as she slipped the disk into the sleek plastic player. She had made great progress in cleaning out and renovating Grey Gables, the old Victorian home

Betsy—"Gram," as Annie called her—had bequeathed to Annie, but some stuff just couldn't be discarded like unwanted trash. Betsy and Annie's grandfather, Charles Holden, had also passed down a love of jazz, a love Annie had shared with Wayne.

She began to sway as the notes of Glenn Miller's *In the Mood* spilled into the air. By the time the saxophone had been joined by trumpets and trombones, Annie had grabbed her tea mug from the table and was dancing down the hallway for a refill. The dance continued with less animation as she added a fresh tea bag to her mug, filled her new electric tea kettle with water, and switched on the kettle with a flourish. Turning around as the kettle began its job, Annie found Boots staring up at her.

"What? Haven't you ever seen a woman dance while making a cup of tea before?"

Boots shook her head as if to respond and strolled to her food bowl, mewing.

Annie laughed and poured kibble into the bowl. She watched the cat nibble the food with dainty bites. When the kettle chimed, she poured water into her cup. The dancing resumed while her tea steeped, and she laughed as the cat took refuge under the kitchen table.

"Boots, you do so amuse me," she said before retrieving her mug and heading back to the living room.

Curled on the sofa with her legs tucked under, Annie closed her eyes as the music vibrated through her body. LeeAnn had sent the perfect gift; with the music came memories. They flipped through her mind like pages in a history book—the happiness of LeeAnn and Herb excitedly announcing, over backyard barbecued burgers and lemonade, the impending arrival of twins; and months later, pacing the hospital waiting room while drinking strong, black coffee with Wayne until an exhausted but grinning Herb entered with the news that mother was doing well and children were beautiful and healthy.

Wayne had had plans for the twins—fishing trips, bicycle rides, and kite flying—and he started spoiling John and Joanna as soon as they arrived home from the hospital. Although she had expected to love her grandchildren, she hadn't foreseen the overwhelming joy they brought into their lives.

The bittersweet memories brought more tears to Annie's eyes. Wayne didn't have a chance to fulfill all those dreams with the twins before he was called home to God by a heart attack. But his quirky smile and color-changing eyes lived on in the twins. Those eyes, much like the old seventies-era mood rings that switched colors, morphed from gray to blue to hazel, depending on his disposition.

Engrossed in her reverie longer than she realized, Annie brought the mug of tea to her lips and nearly choked. The hot tea had turned decidedly cool, and it brought her back to the living room in Grey Gables.

Thank goodness LeeAnn was good about calling, sending photos, and emailing; otherwise she'd go crazy being so far from them. A sudden urge to call her daughter swept through Annie as Billie Holiday lamented lost love, singing, "The way you wear your hat; the way you sip your tea; the memory of all that. No, no, they can't take that away from me."

Annie punched in the number, and as Billie's voice

faded and the CD stopped spinning, LeeAnn answered the phone.

"Mom! How are you?"

"Oh, LeeAnn, the CDs were such a marvelous surprise! I just had to call and tell you how much I'm enjoying listening to them."

"When did they get there? I took the package to the post office after I dropped the twins off at school on Thursday. I've been dying to call you, but I figured you'd let me know."

When did LeeAnn's Southern accent get so thick? Annie glanced at the grandfather clock. "Oh, the postman delivered it about an hour or so ago. I've been listening to it ever since. The songs sent me on a trip down memory lane and had me daydreaming of the day you and Herb told us we were to be grandparents—of twins! Has it really been more than eight years?"

LeeAnn chuckled. "Yep. Remember the crazy names Herb and Dad kicked around that night—Chip and Dip, Tater and Mayo, Ham and Burger?"

"How could I forget?" Annie asked, wiping happy tears from her eyes. "How are our little condiments, anyway?"

"Sweet and salty," LeeAnn said without missing a beat. "And they are bouncing off walls, wanting to talk to you."

"Oh, put them on, honey. I'd love to hear their voices!"

A bit of confusion ensued before the children came on the line.

"Hi, Grandma!" the twins said in unison.

"What's shakin', bacon?" John's voice piped.

"Not much, little man." Annie smiled. The things kids

pick up at school and on television never ceased to amaze. "Boots and I are just listening to the wind and hoping it doesn't blow Grey Gables out to sea, furnishings and all!"

"For real, Grandma?" John said, his voice filled with disbelief.

"No, not really. But the wind blew me around a bit during my walk earlier this afternoon. So, has baseball season started yet?"

"Just started. I'm on the Rangers this year. We have our pictures taken next Saturday. Do you want one?"

Annie's heart did a little flip-flop. John and Joanna were growing up, and she was missing it.

"Absolutely, I want one! And I want to see some videos from your games. Joanna, are you there, sweetie?"

"Yes, Grandma. I'm here; we're on speaker phone. And Ariel says hi too," she said in a voice much softer and higher pitched than her brother's. "Ariel wants to know if you've finished her sweater. She can't wait to see it, you know."

A bit of guilt crept into Annie as she looked at the unfinished fluffy pink dog sweater sticking out of her crochet bag. If she didn't get it done soon, the weather in Texas would be too warm for the little peke-a-poo to wear it until next fall.

"It's getting there. I'll make it a top priority," Annie promised. "How's the dancing going, Joanna?"

"Swimmingly," she replied with a flourish. "I talked Mom into letting me take ballet *and* jazz. I *love* to dance. Oh, Mama wants to talk to you, again. Gotta go. I love you, Grandma!"

"Me too," John chimed in.

"I love y'all too!" Annie replied just in the nick of time before hearing a click as LeeAnn took the phone off speaker to talk privately with her mother.

"They really miss you, Mom. We all do."

Annie could tell significant tongue biting was happening on the other end of the line. LeeAnn was making a concentrated effort to refrain from nagging her about returning to Texas.

"But isn't it great to have cellphones and speaker phones and email and instant messaging?" Annie replied, hoping her words sounded lighthearted. The last thing she wanted was an argument about her decision to remain in Stony Point.

LeeAnn sighed. "I need to get going, Mom. But we'll talk soon, OK? I'm really glad you like the CDs."

"I love the CDs," Annie said. "In fact, I'm going to listen to another one of them while I eat dinner. And I love you too! Bye for now."

Annie put on the second CD of the jazz set, turned up the volume, and headed back to the kitchen, switching on more lights as she walked from the living room down the hall to the kitchen. Late afternoon had turned to darkened early evening, and her growling stomach wanted sustenance as surely as her soul craved the music.

Opting for expediency, Annie ladled leftover home-made vegetable soup into a pottery bowl and put it in the microwave to heat. *A wonderful invention, the microwave*, she thought. *Whatever did people do without it?* By the time she had set a place at the table, fixed a glass of ice water, and fetched a box of oyster crackers from the cupboard, the microwave wizard had worked its magic. Dinner was ready.

Louis Armstrong's punchy trumpet tone on *Stompin' at the Savoy* filtered into the kitchen, bringing a smile to her lips. *Wow! He sure could play that trumpet! What a perfect match with Ella Fitzgerald. They just don't make music like that anymore*, Annie thought.

Several tunes later, Annie rinsed her dishes in the sink, turned off the kitchen light, and settled in the living room for more jazz. Remembering Joanna's question about Ariel's sweater, Annie reached for her crochet bag, determined to finish and mail the peke-a-poo's dainty pink sweater by the end of the week.

Ariel. The name Joanna had picked for the family pet gave her a sense of déjà vu. LeeAnn, who had been about Joanna's age when Disney's animated film *The Little Mermaid* was first released, had named her goldfish after the young mermaid who had wished to become human and marry her handsome prince. LeeAnn had passed her infatuation with mermaids on to Joanna, who had amassed her own collection of the mythical half-woman, half-fish creatures.

"A dog named after a mermaid. I find that quite amusing, don't you?" she asked Boots, who cocked her head as if befuddled by the question.

The CD ended, but Annie continued creating loop after pink loop until the phone's ring pierced the silence.

"Hello?"

"Hello, dahling," said Alice in her best impression of a glamorous Hollywood star of the 1940s. "Would you perhaps be available to breakfast at The Cup & Saucer with your dear old friend tomorrow?"

"Oh, let me check my schedule, dearie. I must not

overbook. I'm frightfully in demand, you know," Annie replied, attempting to stifle a laugh. "I think I can work you in."

Alice chuckled and returned to her native Maine accent. "I'll pick you up at nine o'clock. That should give us enough time to eat, catch up, and still slide into A Stitch in Time for the Hook and Needle Club meeting. Will that work for you?"

"Yes indeed," Annie replied. "I'll be ready and waiting when you arrive in your chariot. But now I'm going to work a bit more on Ariel's sweater before heading to bed. I look forward to breakfast, dahling."

Annie hung up the phone and picked up the sweater in progress, marveling at God's ability to soften great loss with blessings. Losing Gram so soon after Wayne's death was almost too much to bear. But leaving her family in Texas and returning to Stony Point to put Gram's affairs in order also brought a reunion with Alice, her constant companion during childhood summers spent with her grandparents in their rambling old Victorian-era home.

When sleepiness set in, Annie carefully placed her crochet supplies and the sweater in the bag.

"I've made good progress," she told Boots, who was bathing nearby on the braided rug with one leg poised over her head. "Would you like a cute pink sweater to wear in cold weather?"

The cat's leg immediately lowered. With narrowed eyes and twitching ears, she groaned a meow and dashed out of the room, leaving a laughing Annie behind to turn off lights before heading upstairs to bed.

~ 2 ~

Navy Hospital Corpsman Charles Holden collapsed on his bunk, too tired to take off his shoes. He should be caring for the wounded—the bloodied but breathing men struggling to survive as they clung to life in the belly of the ship. He hadn't wanted to leave them, but orders were orders. His commanding officer had told him to get some shut-eye. After eighteen hours of tending the wounded and the dying, he knew his reflexes weren't what they should be. His CO was right; he was more of a hindrance than a help in his current state.

His eyelids closed, but his ears still heard the cries, and visions of shattered limbs and vacant eyes wouldn't leave him. Many of these men, he knew, would never see home again. When would he see the family farm in Connecticut? Smell fresh-cut hay? Taste his mother's beef stew? Hear the roar of his dad's tractor? How long would the constant stream of wounded flow into the ship? And when would the waters off the coast of the Philippine Islands be far behind him?

Sleep wouldn't come. He rolled on his side, trying to count backward from one hundred in hopes of banishing the horror in his head. Reaching zero, he returned to his back.

"I thought you'd be asleep by now."

Startled, Charlie looked up to see his buddy, Mike, standing at the foot of his bunk.

"Couldn't sleep."

"You said to wake you if the lanky chest wound regained consciousness," Mike said, stifling a yawn. "His eyes flickered a bit. He wasn't coherent enough to give him water. He's stirring."

Charlie sat up. "Think he'll make it?"

"Hard to say. I guess we'll find out soon enough. Just what is so special about this one?"

Charlie swung his legs off the bunk. "Honestly, I don't know. He just has—an aura about him."

"With all due respect, I think you need some shut-eye, Charlie."

"Very funny. I'll get some sleep after I check on the patient."

Charlie was soon walking among the rows of wounded soldiers. He stopped at the bedside of a slim, gaunt young man who appeared to be not much younger than he was. The soldier's eyelids fluttered and opened, the only movement on the bruised and battered face.

Charlie tried to hide his amazement. After two days of watching the soldier hover between this world and the next, he smiled and exhaled in relief. Maybe he would make it.

"What's your name?" Charlie asked, his lips close to the soldier's ear.

"Shooter. My friends call me Shooter," the raspy voice whispered before drifting back to sleep.

"Sure thing, Shooter," Charlie murmured as he placed

his fingers on the man's right wrist to check his pulse. "I'll be back to check on you in the morning."

Charlie returned to his bunk, this time stopping to remove his shoes and stripping to his skivvies before sliding under the sheet.

"Dear God," he prayed, silently, "please watch over Shooter and keep him and all the others safe. Calm their fears and give them hope. Grant me the skill and knowledge to heal their wounds. Guide them safely home. Amen."

Soon he was asleep.

Long before daybreak, Charlie was back among the wounded, slowly walking from bunk to bunk and checking the vital signs—body temperature, pulse, blood pressure, and respiratory rate—for each patient.

"Shooter, aren't you a sight for sore eyes?" Charlie joked as he found the soldier sitting up and attempting to drink water.

Shooter grimaced.

"If I look the way I feel, the sight of me could ruin your eyes."

Charlie smiled. The man had a sense of humor.

"Do you remember what happened?" Charlie asked in part to test the man's memory but also to find out a bit about him.

"Not much, really. I know I'm lucky to be here. We were defending the airstrip. Japanese kept shelling. One minute I'm praying, and the next an explosion rips through my chest."

Blood began to seep through the bandage wrapping Shooter's torso.

"Where you from, Shooter?" Charlie kept talking, an attempt to hide his growing concern while loosening the moistening bandages.

"The Midwest." Shooter groaned when the bandage separated from his body, pulling his skin. "I was in school at Ohio University when Uncle Sam came a-calling. I have sort of a yearning to settle in New York, though."

"The City?"

Shooter nodded.

"Why?" Charlie hoped the questions would take Shooter's mind off the pain.

"Curiosity, I suppose. And the music. I've heard they play jazz all night long." Shooter sighed. "Now, that I'd like to hear."

"Jazz. All night? I'd like to hear that too." He wondered if the music could sound as beautiful as crickets on a New England night, a breeze rustling through treetops, or the soft clucking of the hens in the henhouse.

Satisfied the blood wasn't a sign of the soldier's worsening condition, Charlie wrapped a clean bandage around Shooter's chest and promised to return later in the day. "I want to hear more about your plans for New York City."

"It'll be your turn to share, next time," Shooter said, slowly closing his eyes and drifting off to sleep.

*   *   *   *

The bell on the door jangled as Annie and Alice stepped inside The Cup & Saucer.

Alice inhaled and released the breath with an exaggerated moan of ecstasy. "Oh, I feel like pancakes today," she said, eyeing a plate of the tantalizing breakfast treat decked out with melting butter and whipped cream on a nearby table.

"Funny, you don't look fluffy and round to me," Annie teased.

Alice didn't miss a beat. "But I might—if I keep eating pancakes like they're going out of style." She tore her eyes from the pancake plate and searched for a table.

Peggy Carson, attired in her pink waitress uniform and sensible shoes, looked just a bit frazzled as she breezed up and nodded at a recently vacated corner booth.

"Hi, you two! Have a seat. I'll be there to wipe off the table in a jiff just as soon as I unload these," she said, hoisting four egg-laden plates lined up her arms.

"How do you suppose she does that without depositing eggs and bacon on the floor?" Alice asked, watching with obvious admiration as Peggy maneuvered through the crowded tables.

Annie moved toward the corner booth. "Impressive strength and coordination," she said.

The two women slid into the dark green vinyl seats just as a large group of people walked in the door of the already crowded diner.

"I do believe everyone in Stony Point had the same idea this morning," Annie said, looking at her watch. "I hope we get our food quickly enough to make it to A Stitch in Time … on time."

Peggy dashed up on cue with a rag in one hand and two cups on saucers balancing on the other. "I'm glad a table was available for you. It's been nonstop for two hours." She wiped the table with several quick strokes and placed the coffee cups at each place.

"I'm glad too. If we'd have waited too long, Alice might have swiped pancakes right off a plate you were delivering to another customer," Annie teased.

Alice laughed. "Moi? Would I do a thing like that?"

"You'd have to catch me first." Peggy grinned and reached into her apron for two sets of silverware and placed them on the table. "I'll be back with your coffee."

Annie and Alice watched Peggy cross the room to the drink station and grab a coffeepot. She returned in a matter of seconds.

"Two coffees?" Peggy began pouring the steamy liquid into the cup nearest Annie before she nodded. "FYI, we have a new project waiting for the Hook and Needle Club. Betcha don't know what it is."

"Betcha we do too!" Alice quipped.

"We do?" Annie looked confused.

Disappointment clouded Peggy's eyes for a second. "You do? I thought nobody knew yet, but—" Peggy stopped talking when Alice burst out laughing.

"Just kidding. Sorry, I just couldn't resist!" said Alice, stirring a packet of sugar into her coffee, a sly smile curling her lips.

Peggy recovered her composure and grinned.

"You really had me going there for a moment. I'll be back for your order in a sec."

Annie and Alice watched Peggy cheerfully pour coffee at the next table. Still chuckling, Annie leaned across the table and playfully slapped at her friend's arm. "You are so bad!" she teased.

"Yes, but that's what you love about me." Alice's eyes danced beneath her auburn hair. "So what do you suppose this new project is, anyway?"

"Oh, I expect we will know something before we finish our breakfast," Annie said as Peggy returned with her pad and pen in hand.

"Now that everyone finally has coffee, I can get your order," Peggy said.

Peggy quickly jotted down their request—a short stack of pancakes for Alice and a poached egg on rye toast for Annie. She raised her eyes from the pad.

"Any bacon, sausage, ham?"

"No, thank you," the friends said in unison.

With that, Peggy was off in a flash to hang their order in the cook's window behind the counter.

Annie tore one corner from a sugar packet, perched it over her coffee cup, and tapped it three times.

Alice grinned. "Eleven grains of sugar. Why do you bother?"

"Because eleven grains of sugar and a dab of milk make the perfect cup of coffee." Annie tilted a cow-shaped pitcher over her cup and watched a single splash of milk hit the dark liquid.

Alice shook her head. "Do you think you'll have your granddog's sweater done before whatever this new project is that has Peggy about to burst?"

"I made some good headway on it yesterday," Annie said with a shrug. "I also called LeeAnn and the kids, and Joanna said Ariel is most anxious to have her new duds."

Alice laughed. "Somehow I doubt that dog is waiting with bated breath for that sweater!"

"Probably not, but Joanna's really excited, so I'm making a concentrated effort to have it completed and shipped by the end of the week. Sooner, if I can manage it." Annie took a tentative sip of coffee followed by a larger swig.

"Make sure you have LeeAnn send you a photo of the pooch in the sweater. I've gotta see the delight in that dog's eyes!" Alice was clearly amused.

"Oh, something tells me Joanna will badger her mom until photos are taken and emailed to Grandma." Annie smiled at the thought of her granddaughter's excitement about the dog sweater, however humorous it was to Alice.

The two women chattered with the ease of good friends, flowing seamlessly from a conversation about LeeAnn's surprise gift and Annie's love of jazz to Alice's hectic schedule balancing Princessa jewelry and Divine Décor home parties to pay the bills.

"Here we go." Peggy's voice cut into their conversation as she placed assorted dishes on the table, listing the items on each plate.

Annie reached for the pink pig-shaped pepper shaker and sprinkled a light dusting of flakes over her egg while Alice took a sip of her coffee.

Peggy hovered a few seconds longer than necessary as her friends began eating. "Have you heard about the poor Polk family?" she asked, waiting a mere split second before continuing. "Matthew, the youngest son, was diagnosed with a rare eye disease and needs surgery. But with the way hours have been cut at the paper mill, money is tight. Even with Tinia's teaching assistant salary, they're just getting by. And now this? I just don't know what they're going to do!"

Annie and Alice put down their respective forks and looked up at Peggy.

"Wow, that's tough." Alice briefly closed her eyes and shook her head slightly. "I have a difficult time making ends meet, and it's just me! I'm not sure how I'd swing an eye surgery right now."

Annie remembered when LeeAnn had come down with a triple infection in third grade and landed in the Children's Medical Center in Dallas for a week. LeeAnn was a trooper, but it was such a scary time. Annie felt bad for the Polk family.

"I'm so sorry to hear that," Annie said. "How old is Matthew?"

"About eight, I think, just a bit younger than my Emily, and cute as a button!"

"I'll keep the entire family in my prayers. Thanks for letting us know." Annie looked at her watch and picked up her fork.

The breakfast rush was now over, and the roar in the diner quieted.

"I guess we'd best finish breakfast and head to the meeting," Alice said. "We don't want to be late."

Alice and Annie watched Peggy scamper to the drink station and grab the coffeepot once again.

"That girl is good at what she does," Alice mused.

Annie speared a bite of toast and egg on her fork. "Yep! Food and information. What would we do without her?"

The question hung in the air unanswered as the women

quickly finished eating. Annie glanced at the big black-and-white clock on the wall over Alice's shoulder.

"Hmm, are you feeling like a stuffed pancake now?" Annie asked, looking at Alice's empty plate.

Alice chuckled, wiped her mouth with a napkin, and plopped it beside the plate. "I'm now properly fueled for the day! How about you? Ready to get going?"

Annie nodded, took one last sip of coffee, and stood up before placing a couple of dollar bills on the table. "Yeppie, as Joanna would say."

They paid the check and walked toward the door.

"I'll be there soon," Peggy called out as she placed the coffeepot on its burner at the drink station.

As Annie opened the door to leave the diner, she remembered Peggy had mentioned a new project but didn't explain what it was. "Peggy is such a tease," she said with a laugh to Alice as they walked outside onto the sidewalk. "She hinted about a new project, but she never got around to telling us what it was before she went on to telling us about Matthew Polk. I guess we'll find out soon enough."

Seconds after walking out one door, the pair entered another at A Stitch in Time. Neither the shop owner, Mary Beth Brock, nor her employee, Kate Stevens, was in sight. Kate's daughter Vanessa was busy adding a wooden office chair to the circle of comfy chairs where the Hook and Needle Club meeting was held.

"Good morning, Vanessa," said Annie, noticing how meticulously the teenager placed each chair the same distance apart from the next. "How are you?"

Alice appeared confused. "Hi, Vanessa. Shouldn't you be in school?"

"Oh! Hi, Mrs. Dawson and Mrs. MacFarlane." Vanessa, her long brown hair spilling off her shoulders, braced herself with one hand on a chair as she reached over to pull another one closer. "I'm here on official student council business. I'll head back to class after I talk to the group about our upcoming fundraiser."

"Where's your mom?" Annie and Alice asked in unison, as if reading each other's mind—just like they had as kids during Annie's summer visits.

"Here I am!" Kate popped up from behind the cash register. "I was dusting the bag shelves. Mary Beth is in the back, unpacking a shipment of yarn. We have some new spring colors."

"I see." Alice looked around the shop in amusement. Inspired by the changing season, Mary Beth had recently filled large round baskets with new, lighter colors of embroidery thread and shelves with how-to books for spring projects. Clothing items in seasonal fabric were prominently displayed on mannequins. "Just where is she going to put it?"

Kate laughed. "I'm not sure, but she'll find the perfect place. She always does."

Mary Beth emerged from the door to the stockroom, her face partially hidden by the boxes in her arms. "I thought I heard more voices out here. Good morning!"

Vanessa dashed to Mary Beth, reaching her just as the top box began tumbling toward the floor.

"Great catch!" said Mary Beth, taking a few steps before crouching to place the remaining boxes on the floor next to a shelf of yarn skeins. She stood up, tugged on her striped blouse to straighten it, and ran fingers through her short gray hair.

Vanessa placed her box next to the first one and then sat in the wooden chair she had added to the circle of chairs, where Annie and Alice had both taken seats.

Mary Beth began pulling yarn out of one box and placing skeins of the new special spring colors—pea pod, coral rose, honeysuckle, silver cloud, and lavender—on a shelf. "Oh, I just love these bright, cheerful colors," she said.

The wind swept a bit of debris into the shop as Gwendolyn Palmer entered. She lifted a pine green knitted cap from her perfectly coiffed blond hair. The heels of her stylish tan boots clicked on the entryway tile as she moved toward the circle of friends.

"I was afraid I'd not make it here in time. The new housekeeper was late this morning," she explained, placing her knitting bag on the floor while lowering herself into a chair. "But I see I am not the only one running behind."

Mary Beth and Kate had joined the circle. Two chairs were empty.

"Peggy was finishing up a busy breakfast shift at the diner. She'll be here." Alice paused slightly, her eyes twinkling with amusement. "She was bursting with information to share."

Stella Brickson was the next to arrive. The regal octogenarian stepped through the door as her longtime chauffeur, Jason, held it open for her. Despite the wind, every gray hair remained in place, falling in layers around her well-lined face.

"If you're all right then, I'll be back to collect you in an hour," Jason said, one arm on the door and the other firmly in his employer's grasp while she crossed the threshold.

"Yes, Jason, I'll see you in an hour. Sharp." Her curt words would sound harsh to some, but even Annie, the relative newcomer to the group, could see the tender look in Stella's eyes when she spoke to her driver.

Annie noticed that Jason hovered a bit outside the door, as always, watching to make sure Stella made it to her chair before he returned to the white Lincoln Continental she knew would be parked down the street.

"Stella, how do you manage to stay so pulled together on a day as blustery as this?" Annie quipped, rising from her chair and crossing the room to see if the older woman needed help.

She didn't.

"Practice and preparation—always." Stella might move slowly, but her tongue was consistently sharp and razor quick.

As Stella and Annie settled into their seats, Peggy hurried in through the door, shrugged out of her tan coat, and plopped into the remaining chair in the circle.

"I'm finally here!" she announced.

"Yes, we see that," said Stella as each woman pulled a needlework project from her bag.

Annie's sweater for the unsuspecting Ariel drew laughter from the circle of friends. "You haven't finished that dog's sweater yet? Soon it'll be too hot for her to wear it," said Kate, who was taking a break from crocheting one of her colorful, intricate jackets to make a dozen pot scrubbers for a friend who just couldn't live without them.

"I'm working on it. I've been a tad busy," said Annie without explanation.

Alice, her embroidery needle poised midstitch above a partially completed cluster of shamrocks on a bread-basket cloth, snickered. "Thank goodness, for Ariel's sake! Nothing against your crocheted creation, but no dog should have to wear something as undignified as a fluffy pink sweater—not even a peke-a-poo!"

"But we digress," Kate interrupted. "Vanessa would like to talk to us about her friend, Marie Polk, and her little brother. She has an idea to help the family pay for little Matthew's surgery."

Vanessa tossed her long locks behind her shoulders and leaned forward in her chair. "Money is so tight, and Mr. and Mrs. Polk are worried about how they are going to pay all of their regular bills and swing Matthew's surgery too," she explained, glancing at each woman in the circle. "So our student council is holding a fundraiser at the community center at the end of the month. We plan to collect and sell rummage items, baked goods, and homemade crafts. When I told Mom about it, she said the Hook and Needle Club might be able to help."

Peggy grinned, clearly satisfied that she had broken the news to Annie and Alice before Vanessa. She was the first to offer help.

"I don't know what I would do if my Emily had to have surgery," Peggy said. "I just finished cutting out squares of material with Noah's Ark and animals. I can make a child's quilt in time for the fundraiser. And maybe the diner can donate a pie or two."

Each woman agreed to create some sort of handmade item plus a baked good. Annie offered to use a bit of the rhubarb she had frozen the previous summer to bake a pie using Betsy's famous recipe, in addition to crocheting a set of colorful coasters.

"Yum!" Alice rubbed her hands together in delight. "I loved Betsy's rhubarb pie."

Gwen and Stella, both knitters, said they would think about it and decide what to make by the next meeting.

"Annie, are you going to rummage around the attic for a new mystery to serve up with the pie?" asked Gwen, causing a twittering among the women.

Annie chuckled. "I'm more than happy to find rummage items, but I plan to keep the mysteries at bay for awhile. After all, I need to spend time working on the coasters and rounding up the pie recipe."

"Ahem!" Alice said, making all eyes turn her way. "What she means is she will begin working on the coasters as soon as the poor, unfortunate canine in Texas receives her ploofy sweater!"

Laughter filled the shop.

— 3 —

*T*he computer made a loud clicking noise, sounding a bit like it was preparing for liftoff into the wild blue yonder. Annie stared at the blank blue screen and cringed.

"This doesn't look or sound good," she muttered.

Deciding to reboot the computer, she depressed the Ctrl, Alt, and Delete keys, but there was no response. So she held down the power button until the machine fell silent. Then she pressed the power button and said a little prayer.

"Thank you, Lord." Annie listened for the clicking sound as the computer fired up again. But this time its familiar whirring was accompanied by a flip to her email log-in page.

She typed in her email address and password to discover several new additions to her inbox—an electronic newsletter from her church back in Brookfield, Texas, which she scanned quickly for news of old friends; a notice of sale items from an online needlework store; and a short reminder from Vanessa about the fundraiser for the Polk family. Three pieces of junk mail were deleted immediately without being opened.

Leaving the computer running in case she needed it later, Annie decided to peruse her growing collection of crochet pattern books for the right coasters to make for the fundraiser. She flipped through several volumes, searching for a pattern both simple and attractive. A simple design would allow her to complete several sets before the fundraiser, which was to be held in less than three weeks. But she also wanted something attractive enough to bring a fair price and a number of buyers.

The design names made her smile. A pattern called "Dragon Coasters" looked fairly easy and had attractive scalloped edges. But why the "Dragon" name? The simple swirled pastel colors of the "Candied Coasters" reminded her of the cotton candy Gram purchased for her at a fair in Stony Point years ago. And the pinwheel design was different and drew the eye in toward the center of the circle. So many choices!

But the coaster design aptly named "Nature Star" perfectly suited her requirements. Described as "easy" to make, it had the dainty look of a doily but was touted as absorbent enough to protect a tabletop from glass rings.

A quick glance at the pattern solidified her decision: Several sets could easily be made before the fundraiser. She set aside the pattern book it was in to take with her to A Stitch in Time.

She glanced at the computer clock; it was already eleven fifteen. Could it really be nearly lunchtime? Luckily, her breakfast of scrambled eggs and a bowl of oatmeal was substantial enough to hold her for awhile. There was still time to head downtown to purchase yarn for the coasters and a few groceries before hunger would strike.

Grabbing the pattern book and putting it in her project bag, Annie crossed the house to the kitchen to get the purse she had left hanging on a chair back. She picked up the grocery list she had written while eating breakfast and put it in her purse.

Passing through the mudroom, she put on her all-weather jacket before braving the wind whipping between the house and her trusty Chevy Malibu, its burgundy paint contrasting with the brown, winter-worn grass.

Annie had come to love all of the seasons in Maine, each with its quirks and blessings. But she had to admit that she was growing tired of the ceaseless, bone-chilling wind. She looked forward to seeing the yellow and red tulips and purple crocuses peeking out from the ground, and she longed for the lilac bushes to break out in aromatic blooms.

Her mind was still on the coming of spring as she pulled into the parking place right in front of A Stitch in Time. Perhaps choosing bright colors for the coaster project would help fill her need for warmth and color until flowers began appearing around Stony Point.

She found Mary Beth and Kate poring through needle-craft books in search of items to make for the Polk family fundraiser.

"Hi, ya'll. How's your day going?" Annie's Southern drawl no longer drew snickers from local New Englanders. Instead, the two women greeted her with warm smiles.

"Slow, business-wise. But that's OK because we have time to decide what to make for the fundraiser," Mary Beth replied. "We're having a hard time choosing."

Annie pulled the book with the pattern for the "Nature Star" coasters from her project bag. "I found these going through my pattern books this morning. I'd like to do them in several spring colors. I chose an easier pattern so I could complete several sets of six in time for the event. What do you think?" Annie opened the book on the counter for Mary Beth and Kate to see.

Kate, one of the most gifted crochet artisans Annie knew, nodded in approval.

"Well, this is easier than what you normally do," Kate said, "but the pattern has always been one of my favorites. There's something sort of elegant in its simplicity. And you're right; this is easily doable in a short amount of time, especially since you're getting a quick start."

Mary Beth picked up the book and walked over to the shelves she had stocked with yarn the day before.

"What do you think about these?" she said, pulling a skein of each color as she recited their names. "Pea pod, coral rose, honeysuckle, silver cloud, lavender, daffodil yellow."

Annie reached out and touched the lightweight yarn cradled in Mary Beth's arms and smiled.

"These are perfect! I'll take one of each."

Annie followed Mary Beth to the cash register where Kate was waiting to ring up the order.

"Oh, Annie, these colors are gorgeous! You know, we have some small muslin bags left over from the holidays. Mary Beth has them marked down to seventy-five cents each. I'll bet one set of the coasters would fit in each bag."

Upon hearing Kate's words, Mary Beth quickly retrieved six bags from the sale shelf. "I'll sell you these for fifty cents each to further the cause," she said, placing them on the counter.

"Deal!" Annie said, picking up a bag and taking a closer look at it. "What a great idea, Kate."

The three friends chatted about the plight of the Polk family and the upcoming fundraiser.

"Vanessa has such a big heart," Annie said. "I've never seen a teenager with a more positive attitude toward community service and a strong desire to serve others."

Mary Beth, who had never married and didn't have children of her own, had adopted Vanessa as a type of spiritual granddaughter. "Not only is she in student council, on the school honor court, and president of the art club," she said, sounding every bit the proud grandmother, "but she logs record-breaking hours at the animal shelter. I've had so much fun watching her mature into a beautiful young lady, inside and out."

"Thank you," said Kate, always quiet and economical in her word choice.

"Methinks this compassion was instilled in her by a caring mother," Annie said, gently patting Kate's arm. Annie knew how tough it had been for Kate to keep Vanessa grounded in the face of a crumbling marriage and divorce. "You've done such a wonderful job raising her. She is a great kid."

Uncomfortable with the praise, Kate caught her breath while putting Annie's purchases in a large paper bag. "I've had a lot of help and a great support system. I'm thankful to live in a community where folks rally around each other in the hard times and celebrate together in the good ones."

Mary Beth and Annie shared a knowing glance. Kate didn't realize how special she was.

Kate handed Annie her bag of crocheting supplies. "Have fun with your coasters! I'll bet they will be a top seller!"

Grasping the bag, Annie started for the door. "I will, and I'm looking forward to seeing what you two end up making. Bye now!"

"Goodbye!" Mary Beth and Kate said in unison.

Annie stepped out onto the street, clutching the shopping bag in one hand and her car keys in the other. Her heart skipped a beat when she heard a familiar voice call her name. "Annie Dawson, if I didn't know any better, I'd think you were avoiding me!"

Ian Butler, the town's mayor, walked in her direction. He looked quite dashing in tan corduroys, pine green-and-beige sweater, and an unzipped leather bomber jacket. "Well, fancy meeting you here, outside A Stitch in Time! It's great to see you, Annie. I've tried to call …" Ian said, his voice dissipating into the wind.

Annie froze beside her car. "Ian! I'm sorry I've been so difficult to reach lately," she stammered. "Please, don't take it personally."

She placed a hand on his arm and glanced up at him, hoping her windblown hair would hide the color rising in her cheeks and the guilty look in her eyes. She hadn't intended to avoid him; she just didn't know how to handle the changes evolving in their relationship, which had grown in recent months from polite friendship to something more. But the something more had yet to be defined.

"Well, I hear you ladies have a new project brewing, so apology accepted," he said to Annie's relief. "It's a wonderful thing you are doing for the Polk family. I understand you're making a triple contribution, including Betsy's rhubarb pie." He looked into her eyes with a tenderness that left Annie speechless. "You're a blessing to the community, Annie."

"Thank you, that's really sweet, but I'm really just doing the right thing. God calls us all to be servants to others. Anyway, Vanessa deserves the credit. The fundraiser and the Hook and Needle Club's involvement in it were her ideas," Annie said.

She unlocked her car door and tossed the bag onto the passenger seat before turning around to face Ian. "I'm stowing my package in the car while I pick up a few things at Magruder's. Boots will never forgive me if I return home without her favorite food!"

Ian chuckled. "I understand completely. Tartan is rather fond of his rawhide bones. I must make sure I have a replacement ready when I toss out the old ratty bone. If I don't, he pouts."

Annie couldn't envision the high-spirited schnauzer ignoring his owner too long. "What would we do without our four-legged friends to keep us company?" she asked.

"Indeed. Say, Annie, do you have time to lunch with me at Maplehurst Inn? I've just completed a long morning of meetings, and I'm famished." Ian's voice was calm, but his eyes were pleading.

Annie hesitated a second before responding.

"I'd love to, Ian, really I would. But I must get home. I'll take a rain check though!"

"I understand. Another time—soon?" Disappointment tinged his voice. "I miss you, Annie."

She looked into his eyes and saw the flicker of hurt in them. Smiling, she gave him the quickest of hugs and a light kiss on the cheek before crossing the street to Magruder's.

*   *   *   *

Mary Beth and Kate watched Annie close the door and walk several paces to her car.

"Annie has really become a special part of Stony Point, hasn't she?" asked Mary Beth. "It's like she's always lived here."

Kate nodded and walked from behind the counter, taking a few paces toward the door.

"To think I once believed Harry's lies and accused her of flirting with him. I wasn't very nice to her, but she was so kind in return," Kate said, now able to speak of her ex-husband without cringing or wiping away tears.

She felt Mary Beth's arm around her shoulders.

"Annie's heart is filled with love and forgiveness. She's suffered so much with losing Betsy so soon after Wayne's death. It took a while for a lot of us in Stony Point to warm up to her. You weren't the only one. But when we got to know her, we adopted her as one of our own. Everyone has helped her heal, just as they nursed my heart back to health when Clyde broke it all those years ago in New York City." Mary Beth grinned with amusement. "Who knew I'd turn out to be a small-town girl?"

Kate laughed and stared through the glass door, watching Ian's face light up as he crossed the street toward Annie.

"Do you suppose she has any idea how he feels?" Kate mused. "See the way he looks at her? I didn't know a man's face could glow like that!"

"Hmm." Mary Beth dropped her arm, stepped forward, and leaned a bit closer to the glass. "I'm not so sure Annie realizes how *she* feels about *him*. Her eyes are sparkling, but her body looks tense."

Kate closed her eyes and willed herself to not think about Harry and the way he bullied her during their marriage. He had never looked at her the way Ian gazed at Annie. Would anyone ever care for her so much?

Mary Beth stared with obvious disappointment as Annie kissed Ian's cheek and hurried across the street toward the grocery store. Turning to go retrieve boxes of merchandise from the storage room, she was stopped in her tracks by the longing on Kate's face.

"There's someone out there for you too, Kate," she said.

*   *   *   *

Arms laden with grocery bags, Annie fumbled with her keys while unlocking the back door to Grey Gables and nearly stumbled over Boots as she entered the kitchen through the mudroom.

"Yes, Boots, I have your treats." She placed her packages on the kitchen counter and kneeled down to rub under the cat's chin, and was rewarded with a loud, continuous *purr*. "Did you miss me?"

She stood up and quickly put the groceries away, carefully maneuvering around Boots, who seemed to know that a treat was tucked away in one of the bags waiting for her. When she had finished, the thought of lunch was suddenly very appealing.

"You may have your treat after I finish making my sandwich," said Annie as she removed two slices of whole-grain bread from the wrapper and placed them on one of Gram's delicate floral china plates.

The roast beef had looked too good to pass up at Magruder's, so she had grabbed a bit of brie and horseradish to fix her favorite sandwich for lunch.

"*Voilà* ... a masterpiece!" Annie said, her dramatics drawing a blasé look from Boots. "Yes, ma'am, you may have your treat now."

Annie fished a cheesy treat from the zip-top foil bag and stored the rest in the cat's treat canister.

"Here you go. Don't eat it all at once."

While Annie washed her hands, Boots took the treat to her bowl to munch in peace. When the sandwich was gone, Annie sighed and wiped her hands on a pink-and-burgundy cloth napkin. "I believe I'll spend the rest of the day finishing up Ariel's sweater," she told the feline, who was engrossed in crunching her treat.

After washing her lunch dishes, Annie put one of her new jazz CDs in the player and hunkered down on the living room couch, intent on finishing the sweater. Several hours passed quickly. Annie took breaks after each CD finished play—a tea break in midafternoon and light dinner later. With Boots curled up beside her, Annie hooked the last stitch on the sweater just as the final strains of *Moonlight Serenade* faded into silence. Tomorrow she would put on the finishing touches.

Yawning, she placed the dog sweater back in her craft bag. After turning off the CD player and the lamp in the living room, Annie padded into the library to shut down the computer.

As the computer completed its noisy process, Annie studied the portraits hanging on one wall between the desks. From one frame, Betsy and Charlie gazed down at her in their Sunday best. *My, wasn't Grandpa handsome with his dark hair and distinguishing mustache!* The photographer had somehow managed to capture the twinkle in his eye. He caught Gram's lighthearted energy in her warm smile. Whoever took this photo must have known Gram and Grandpa pretty well to have captured their personalities so perfectly.

In the other portrait, they were joined by their young daughter, Judy—Annie's mother—looking a bit like Shirley Temple with her dimples and ringlets. As many times as Annie had looked at the portrait since moving to Stony Point, this was the first time she had noticed how much the twins resembled their grandmother. The photos had faded so much; time and oxidation had taken their toll.

Annie turned off the library lights and headed upstairs, thinking of the portraits and the possibility of having them reprinted or restored. *Where in the world would Gram have stored the negatives?*

— 4 —

There it was. Shooter's home loomed in front of him, a tall brick building close to the street. Not a tree or blade of grass in sight. Charlie loped up the four steps and opened the creaky wood-and-glass door to find several rows of mailboxes. He scanned them looking for Shooter's name. There, 322. Up two flights of stairs.

He rapped on the door three times and waited for it to open.

"Charlie, you made it!" Shooter smiled below the mustache, a new addition since his soldiering days.

"You're a sight for sore eyes, Shooter." The two men shook hands and lightly slapped each other on the shoulder.

Shooter opened the door wider and granted Charlie entry with a flourish of his arm. "My castle, if you will. It's not much, but my couch is all yours. Bunk here as long as you like."

Shooter took Charlie's bag and tossed it into the corner of the living room between a mahogany desk and an old overstuffed chair. Smoke drifted up in curls from the glass ashtray on the coffee table into the soft lamplight.

"Have a seat." Shooter gestured toward the couch as he sat down in the window side chair. "Got your land legs back yet?"

Charlie nodded. "They returned while I was in Washington. It sure is great to be back in the States. It seems like I was gone forever."

"You were, my friend, you were."

The room was silent, the air thick with unspoken words hanging between them—two men who defied death when it was all around them.

"Tomorrow I'll show you the sights." Shooter took a puff on the cigarette. "Hey—are you up for a trip to my favorite club, The Avant-Garde, right now?"

"It's the main reason I came to New York." Charlie was relieved to be joshing with his friend. "You just happen to be here."

The two friends laughed easily as they walked several blocks through New York's West Village. Shooter described his recuperation in Ohio after leaving Charlie aboard the USS Beneficent.

"You didn't take very long to make it to New York," said Charlie.

"I simply followed the music, my boy; I just had to find the beat."

Shooter's Midwestern accent and easy-going manner lurked behind a newly acquired worldliness. He had become a New Yorker.

Charlie stood before The Avant-Garde and raised his eyebrows. The narrow building stood sandwiched between a tailor's shop and a five-and-dime store, its green door hidden in shadows beyond neon lights. Shooter grinned and opened the door without saying a word. After a short hallway, Charlie followed Shooter down a stairway; the club was dark, smoke-filled, and humming with electricity.

"What's buzzin', cousin?" A hand clapped Shooter on the shoulder.

"Just showing my buddy Charlie here a good time." Shooter glanced from one man to the other. "Mitchell, meet Charlie Holden, the man who saved my life in the South Pacific. Charlie, Mitchell Grants. His family owns this fine establishment."

Mitchell flashed a toothy grin and held out his hand. "You're a lucky man, Charlie. Yardbird is playing tonight."

"Yardbird?"

"Charlie Parker. Some people think he's the world's best sax player." Mitchell glanced at Shooter and back to Charlie. "Did you really save Shooter's life?"

"Well, I only …."

"He brought me back from the brink of death on a ship stinking with it."

Charlie shifted from one foot to the other and looked at the floor. "Shooter, I was only doing my job as a corpsman. I …."

"That's good enough for me." Mitchell pumped Charlie's hand again. "Have a round on the house—a thank-you for sending our friend Shooter back to American soil in one piece."

"Thank you," Charlie said, "that's mighty nice of you."

The Avant-Garde wasn't fancy, but something in the way people moved purposely to their seats filled Charlie with anticipation. The world's best saxophone player. Charlie knew, after nearly three years in the Pacific, just how large the world really was; and the best in the world was right here in this narrow little building three blocks from Shooter's apartment.

He followed his friend to a tiny table just off the corner of the stage.

Shooter leaned into the table. "Look in the wings to the right of the stage. There he is—that's Yardbird Parker."

The musician was leaning with his back and head against the wall with the horn perched on one knee. A light from beyond the open backstage door created a hazy silhouette.

Mitchell appeared at the table with two glasses in his hands. "Enjoy the show."

The noise level rose as the crowd chattered with anticipation when several band members strolled onstage. Just as Mitchell turned to head back to the club's entrance, a slow drum cadence reverberated through the room, and suddenly Yardbird was onstage.

At that moment, Charlie knew there was no other place on earth he'd rather be.

*   *   *   *

"Oh, Boots, it's you!" Annie woke with a start after a fitful night of sleep to find the cat stretched out on the pillow beside her, a furry gray tail tickling her nose.

Boots lifted her head and glanced back at Annie with a look that said, "It's about time you woke up."

"Are you hungry, Miss Boots?" Annie stretched as much as she could without disturbing the cat.

With Annie now wide awake, the feline maneuvered her body so she could rub her face along Annie's cheek. A meow was followed by intense purring.

"You're mellowing in your old age, my girl." Annie lifted her head on one elbow and reached out the other arm to stroke under the cat's chin with her index and middle fingers. "Let's get breakfast."

Annie yawned and rolled out of bed just as Boots ran out the bedroom door. She exchanged her red long-sleeved nightshirt—the one John and Joanna had given her last Christmas because the moose on the front reminded them of Maine—for jeans and a sweatshirt.

By the time Annie entered the kitchen, Boots was already staring at her food bowl in anticipation of breakfast.

"Hold your horses, Boots, while I put on water to boil for my oatmeal." Annie measured a cup of water into a small saucepan. She added a dash of salt before putting it on the stove to heat. Then she scooped a serving of oatmeal into a measuring cup and set it on the counter next to the stove.

Meow! Boots swished her tail back and forth, and glared at Annie.

"Yes, ma'am. It's coming." Annie grabbed the cat's pottery bowl and put it on the counter before taking the remains of a can of savory beef cat food from the refrigerator and a scoop of dry kibble from a large can by the mudroom door. "You are one spoiled cat, Boots," Annie said, scraping the beef into the food bowl and slightly heating it in the microwave before pouring the kibble on top. "But I sure do love having you around!"

She placed the bowl on top of the mat that designated the cat's dining area. Boots attacked her food with dainty abandon as Annie washed her hands and stirred the oats into the boiling water.

By the time Boots had finished her breakfast, Annie was folding a little butter, brown sugar, and raisins into her own.

She sat down at the table and contemplated where to look for the portrait negatives. Where would Gram have put them for safekeeping? Renovations had been done in almost every room of the house. Why hadn't they turned up already?

She ran through the series of renovation projects completed inside Grey Gables since she had arrived in Stony Point. The first floor was largely completed. The kitchen cabinets were totally redone with glass fronts, so they couldn't be hiding there. Ditto the bookshelves in the library. Surely Gram wouldn't have kept them in the attic, where the temperature fluctuated with the seasons. Perhaps they were lurking on the second floor, where Annie still had a few nooks and crannies left to explore—under the beds, a linen closet here, a wood chest there. The guest room could be a good place to start.

Boots had taken off for parts unknown in the old creaking house by the time Annie had rinsed out her bowl, retrieved the cordless phone off its cradle, and climbed the stairs to the guest room. Standing in the doorway, she surveyed the room. What would she find under the bed?

She crossed the room and dropped to her knees between the dresser and bed. Three large rectangular clear plastic containers filled the space under the box springs. They were labeled in Gram's neat, slanted handwriting, "Fabric Remnants," "Yarn," and "Dress-Up Clothes."

Dress-up clothes? Hadn't all of Gram's old dress clothes already been taken to the church for needy families? Sitting cross-legged on the floor, Annie pulled the clothing-filled box toward her and removed the lid. Lifting the top garment, a scoop-necked navy blue dress with red piping, she sighed and rubbed the embroidered stars on the square collar. "Gram, you kept this all these years?"

Annie reached for the phone she had tossed on the bed and pushed the speed-dial number for Alice.

"Hi, Annie! What are you doing on this fine windy day?"

"You are never going to guess what I found in the guest room," Annie said, spreading out the dress on the comforter. "Oh—hi, by the way."

"Umm, hidden treasure left by the old sea captain who built the place?"

"A treasure, yes, but not gold and jewels. I found our stash of dress-up clothes, including—"

"The blue star-embroidered dress!" Alice finished for her, squealing like a child. "I get to wear it first!"

Years fell away while the two friends remembered long hours of playing dress-up during seemingly endless rainy days.

"How we bickered over who would wear that dress!" Annie said, her voice ringing with laughter. "You'd stand there with your flaming hair, hands on your hips, and insist your auburn hair would highlight the red stars."

"Yep, and I would feel very convincing until you fired back with your trump card. How could I possibly justify my right to wear the dress your grandmother was wearing the first time she danced with your Grandpa Holden at that USO dance in Stony Point?" Alice snickered. "I guess all is fair in love and dress-up."

"I wasn't so amused when Gram made me let you wear the dress," Annie countered. "It was so like her to make us take turns. She wanted you to feel special too."

"I did, Annie, I did," Alice said. "But look at the time!

As much as I've loved tripping down memory lane with you, I must head to Petersgrove for a combination ladies brunch and Divine Décor party. Thirty-five people are attending this one; sounds promising!"

"May you have a fruitful party, then! Hopefully I'll be productive as well. I'm looking for the negatives for the portraits of Gram and Grandpa. I want to have them reprinted."

"Good luck with your search. Talk to you soon. Bye!"

"Adios, mi amiga." Annie switched off the phone and tossed it on the bed.

Annie folded the treasured dress and put it back in the dress-up container. Satisfied the negatives weren't under the bed, she replaced the lid and returned the storage bins to their original spot.

Where to look next? she thought. She had cleaned out the drawers and closets in the room before the last time that LeeAnn, Herb, and the twins had visited. How about the chest of drawers in the living room?

After stopping by the kitchen to fix a cup of Orange Zinger tea, Annie stood before the chest of drawers in the living room, wondering if the negatives were in there. Placing her teacup on top of the chest, she opened the first drawer to find several decks of cards, bridge scoring pads, an assortment of pencils and pens, and a set of coasters featuring several Stony Point landmarks, including Butler's Lighthouse, the docks, Maplehurst Inn, and Grey Gables. Betsy and Charlie had been avid bridge players.

Closing the drawer, Annie took a sip of tea before opening the next one. She found an assortment of candle tapers in varying sizes and colors.

"Harrumph, I could have used you during the last storm when the lights died on me. But I know where you are for next time," she mumbled aloud.

Boots sauntered into the room with a look that seemed to say, "Silly human!"

"What? You've never heard anyone talk to candlesticks before?" She closed the drawer as Boots jumped onto the nearby sofa, kneaded the perfect spot, and curled up for a nap.

The deep bottom drawer didn't reveal the negatives either, but Annie squealed in childlike delight when she saw a few of Grandpa's old jazz records stacked inside. Artie Shaw, clarinet in hand, looked up from the first album cover. Glenn Miller and his trombone graced the second, and on the bottom record cover, Grandpa's favorite musician, Charlie Parker, cradled his saxophone.

She took the records over to the huge old stereo, removed the CD player from the top, and opened the lid. Would this old dinosaur work after all these years?

Annie blew the dust off the first album and gingerly removed the vinyl disc from its sleeve. She slipped it onto the turntable, turned the "on" knob, and carefully placed the needle arm on the record.

The familiar notes of Glenn Miller's classic *Little Brown Jug* filtered into the room amid pops and crackles created by the needle crossing the aged vinyl.

Annie picked up her teacup and sat on the couch, petting distance from Boots. Hugging one of Betsy's cross-stitch pillows under one arm, she sipped her tea and thought of two young girls—the redhead clad in starry blue and the blonde in yellow silk with a matching hat—dancing in the center of the room, giggling and creating their own steps. Nearby, Grandpa sat in his easy chair, writing in his journal, as Gram relaxed on the couch, working on a cross-stitch scene. How surprised Annie and Alice had been when Gram and Grandpa joined their dance!

Snapping out of her reverie, Annie drained her teacup, placed the cup and saucer on the coffee table, and leaned back to enjoy the rest of the record. When the final note played and the needle arm returned to its perch, Annie put the record into its sleeve.

"I guess it's back to work for me, Boots."

Ignoring the slight rumble of her empty stomach, Annie padded down the hallway to the library and stood in the doorway. Could the photo negatives be tucked away in a file in the huge old oak desk? Probably not. Most of the files had already been searched while gathering information to settle Gram's estate. The negatives would have been noticed then. Where would Gram put the negatives? She became a little absentminded just before she passed away, and she always had a book in her hand. Annie scanned over the bookshelves lining the room. Had Gram stuck them between the pages of a book? She groaned. Why did Gram and Grandpa have to be such bibliophiles? There must be hundreds of books here.

Annie spied the old copy of Rudyard Kipling's *Jungle Book* and pulled it from its perch between two other collections of children's stories. She ran her fingers over the embossed title and smiled. How she had loved sitting on Grandpa's lap as he read the tales, adopting a different voice for each character! Closing her eyes, she could almost feel his arms around her and smell the sweet aroma of his cherry-laced pipe tobacco.

"All right, Annie old girl. Put the book away and keep looking!" She returned Kipling to his shelf space and continued to search through the books, seeking a title that jumped out at her, or that seemed out of place. Looking down, she spied a large book about New York City jutting out farther than the other bindings. Leaning closer, she could see something peeking out of the top of the book.

She pulled the book off the shelf and opened it to find several small black-and-white photos stuck between the pages. In one, a young man in his mid to late twenties with short, dark hair gazed upward in amazement at an endless wall of concrete and glass. "Charlie and the Empire State Building. 1945. L.H." was written in neat block style on the back.

What a cool perspective! Annie thought. Whoever took this photo had managed to capture Grandpa's awe and the building's massive size at the same time. Annie marveled at how the photographer had re-created such emotion in a black-and-white photo.

Enthralled with her find, Annie took the book to the window seat, sat down, and reopened it to a different page and another photo. Grandpa, his hair blown by the wind, leaned casually against the railing on the side of a boat as it passed the Statue of Liberty. The caption read, "Charlie eyeing the Lady. Staten Island Ferry. 1945. L.H."

Nineteen forty-five, the year he met Gram. Lady Liberty must have been the last lady he eyed before meeting the love of his life!

Annie placed the picture on the desk next to the first one and flipped the book's pages to the next photo marking a spot. Grandpa, handsome in civilian clothes and a dark jacket, was framed by a massive web of cables and twin arches towering overhead. Was that the Manhattan skyline in the background? "Charlie crossing Brooklyn Bridge. 1945. L.H." was written on the back.

Annie studied the photo and the corresponding page in the book. *Look at all of the people on that bridge!* she thought. *Strolling the bridge must have been as popular in the forties as it is today.*

Annie held the photo up to the window for more light and realized the sun was fading. She glanced at her watch. Seven fifteen! No wonder her stomach was growling; she had spent all day traipsing down memory lane. She stacked the photos on the desk and carried *Scenes of New York City* into the kitchen to read while nibbling on a snack.

Soon Annie was standing in front of the opened refrigerator, wondering what she wanted to eat. Although hungry, nothing in particular looked appetizing.

Smiling, she remembered spending long hours gardening with Gram. They would lose themselves in plants, dirt, water, and sunshine, stopping only when the sun began to sink below the horizon. By then, they would be ravenous but too exhausted to cook a hot meal.

"Gram's special—ahhh—that's what I want!" Annie said as Boots strolled into the kitchen and began making figure eights around her ankles. She pulled a bag of grapes, a brick of cheese, and the roast beef from the refrigerator. Minutes later, she sat down at the kitchen table with a glass of chilled apple juice and a photo-worthy plate of rolled roast beef slices, squares of cheddar cheese, and a bunch of grapes. A slice of Alice's dill bread was tucked between the beef and cheese.

Opening *Scenes of New York City* to the Empire State Building page, she read about the landmark that had amazed her grandfather so many decades earlier. Completed in 1931, the 102-story, art deco-style building had taken under two years to build. Closing her eyes, Annie tried to imagine what her grandfather, a farm boy accustomed to wide-open spaces and fresh air, had felt while gazing at the towering building.

She tore off a bite of bread, placed a slice of cheese on it and popped the morsel into her mouth. Taking a sip of juice, she continued reading.

How appropriate! The land where the Empire State Building now sat was first developed as a farm by a man named John Thompson in the late 1700s. Annie ran her finger along the sentences underlined in ink. Grandpa must have noticed this connection between the building's history and his own. Who would have thought a piece of New York City had been farmland at one time?

The Big Apple came alive to her as she read about the Statue of Liberty, the robed, torch-bearing symbol of freedom keeping vigilant watch in the harbor, and the Brooklyn Bridge, an artery carrying people in and out of the city for decades.

The phone's ring pierced the silence. Wiping her hands on a napkin, she felt an odd mixture of joy and apprehension when she saw the number on the display screen. "Hello, Ian. How are you?"

"Annie! I hope you're staying dry on this rainy day."

"Dry as a bone. I've spent the day traipsing down memory lane after finding all sorts of family treasures—

well, except for the one I was actually looking for." Annie braced the phone between her ear and shoulder, and carried her empty plate and glass to the sink.

"Oh, so did you find another mystery?"

Annie laughed. "No mysteries. But I did find the dress-up clothes Alice and I played with as kids, a stash of Grandpa's old jazz albums, and photos of him taken in New York City."

"Now, I'd like to see a photo of you and Alice in those dress-up clothes," Ian said with a chuckle.

"Oh, we were quite glamorous."

"I imagine so."

Annie could tell he was amused. "So far I've not found any photos of the glamorous Grey Gables Girls, but you'll be first to see them—after Alice, of course—if I do."

"I'll hold you to that. Say, Annie, a bakery looking to expand into Stony Point sent over a basket of delicious-looking goodies today. I thought perhaps I'd bring them over tomorrow morning, and we could have breakfast together. Are you free?"

Annie hesitated a few seconds. She was unsure of her growing feelings for Ian and wondered if seeing him was a good idea. But he made her laugh, and their time together always passed so quickly. "I don't know; I might put you to work in the attic. I still need to find rummage items for the benefit auction, you know. Still interested?"

"That's a risk I'm willing to take. After all, your attic is a microcosm of Stony Point history, and you know how much I love our little town!"

Annie struggled to keep her breathing even. "In that case, can you be here around eight thirty? Bring on the pastries!"

5

Annie's heart quickened when she opened the door to a damp, windblown Ian standing on the front porch.

"Good morning, Ian!" He was handsome, despite running from the car in the wind and rain, which had his thick but neatly trimmed gray hair sticking straight up in some places and lying flat in others. Was she imagining things or was that a sparkle in his eyes?

"Good morning." He reached up with one hand and brushed her hair back from her face. "It's great to see you."

Ian stepped through the door, and Annie closed it behind him. He held out a brown cellophane-wrapped basket sporting a big yellow-and-green bow.

"Compliments of Takes the Cake Bakery," he said with a scintillating smile.

Annie peeked inside the basket, finding a sinful-looking collection of muffins, biscotti, cookies, and what looked like slices of pound cake. "Oh, these look like they might possibly give Alice a run for her money in the baking department!"

She led Ian to the kitchen, where the coffeemaker was just sputtering the last few drops of hazelnut java into the carafe. Two green-tinged pottery mugs and a small matching pitcher of half-and-half sat on the counter beside it.

He inhaled deeply.

"Mmm. That smells good! Is it hazelnut?"

Annie nodded and set the basket of goodies on the kitchen table.

Stepping to the counter, she poured the rich, dark brew into the mugs. "The name is 'Happily Hazelnut.' I found it in a quirky little coffee shop while Christmas shopping in Portland. I pull it out of the freezer for special occasions."

Ian grasped the cup she held out to him and looked into her eyes. "I'm honored to be considered special."

Annie felt her cheeks tingle and suspected they were turning a nice rosy hue.

Coffee in one hand, Ian reached up with the other and gently cupped his hand around Annie's cheek, stroking her jawbone with a feather touch of his thumb.

Her heart thumped a wild beat, the pounding reaching to her ears. Annie held her breath. Gazing up at Ian's face, she was suspended in time as he leaned closer, his eyelids closing as he lowered his lips to hers. Annie relaxed into the kiss, reveling in the warmth of his touch with her own eyes closed, until reality slapped her. What was she doing, kissing another man? Wayne was the love of her life. She was being unfaithful!

Breaking the kiss and stepping from Ian's arms, Annie struggled to maintain composure. An odd mixture of joy and guilt washed over her.

"You're the heartbeat of Stony Point," she said. "Of course you're special." Pulling her gaze from his eyes, she turned to the counter and picked up her own cup of coffee and struggled to sound calm. "Not to mention, you're great at sharing. I can't wait to dig into these treats!"

Ian's eyes flickered with disappointment, and Annie wondered if his insides were quaking as much as hers.

They sat down at Gram's antique oak table where Annie had placed a stick of butter and a brick of cream cheese on two cut-glass plates. Two place settings of silverware were resting on white napkins embroidered with daffodils, the flowers picking up the yellow hue from place mats and the kitchen walls.

Ian removed the bow and peeled back the cellophane from the basket. "Which of these treats shall we try first? I believe this biscotti might be worthy of your Happily Hazelnut. What do you think?"

Annie nodded and held her cup toward Ian. "Here's to Takes the Cake Bakery, great coffee, and—"

"To us!" Ian finished for her.

They lightly touched their mugs together before taking their first sip of coffee.

"Have you ever been to Takes the Cake?" Annie reached for one of the four slices of biscotti leaning along one side of the basket. "Isn't it in Portland?"

"Yes, that's the one," Ian said.

"I remember peeking in a bakery window during our last trek to the Maine Historical Society. Alice, Kate, Gwen, and I came across it while looking for a place to have lunch." Annie pointed at a row of mouthwatering cookies in the basket. "We nearly lost Alice to those decadent-looking chocolate, caramel, and coconut confections."

Ian grabbed a biscotti of his own. "It's owned by two generations of the Laurent family, descended from a long line of bakers. They're looking at opening a small bakery in

Stony Point, offering cookies, pastries, and breads as well as a couple of lunch items per day."

"I wonder if the bakery would be competition for The Cup & Saucer?" Annie asked. "We had this old mom-and-pop diner in Brookfield with great food and lots of local history. Unfortunately, it went out of business when a national chain opened across the street. Would the new bakery be a franchise with a local owner?"

Ian shook his head. "The young Laurent siblings would run the new place while their parents keep the original bakery. It would make a great addition to downtown. I think people in our surrounding towns who have visited the bakery in Portland would drive here for their pastries. The Laurent name is known all over Maine."

Annie dunked the dense, almond-flavored confection in her coffee. "It looked like a cute place. Knowing they might open a store in Stony Point, now I wish we had actually gone inside." She took a bite of biscotti and moaned with delight. "Oh, this is fabulous!"

Ian chuckled, his brown eyes twinkling. "With the frequency of trips you and your friends make to the historical society, I'm sure you will have a chance to visit the bakery before they open one here—if they open one here. Which reminds me, don't you think it's about time for another mystery to appear? It's been awfully quiet around here."

"Bite your tongue!" Annie joked, wiggling her left index finger in a mock warning. "I like quiet. I've been able to catch my breath. Besides, the only mystery I need to solve is finding where in the world Gram stashed the negatives for the portraits in the library. I really want to have them redone."

"Annie, you don't need the negatives in this day and age. If you can't find them, just take the portraits to a digital photographer or graphic designer and have them scanned and enhanced," Ian said. "It should be quick and relatively inexpensive."

"What? You mean take away the thrill of the search?" Annie smiled sheepishly. "I didn't even think of having them scanned."

Ian reached into the basket and plucked out a jumbo muffin and broke it in half before spreading a thin layer of cream cheese over one side. "This one is cranberry and nearly as big as the ones my mother made when I was a kid."

Coffee cup to her lips, Annie peered over the rim and tried to read Ian's expression. Had the kiss affected him too? He also had lost the love of his life suddenly; Arianna had succumbed to a brain aneurism. He didn't seem uncomfortable, but Annie knew that politicians are usually skilled at hiding their feelings. Did he feel unfaithful to Arianna?

"I'm not sure if this is pound cake or dense bread, but it's calling my name," said Annie, setting her cup down and pulling a yellow, crumb-encrusted slice from the basket. "I will have consumed an entire day's worth of carbs at the end of this meal!"

"Have no fear," Ian said, swiping the napkin across his lips. "You wear them well!"

Ian's cellphone rang from its holster on his belt. He checked the number calling. He looked at Annie with an apologetic look. "Excuse me, I have to take this. It's Charlotte."

Annie nibbled on her pound cake and tried not to listen

to Ian's conversation with his longtime secretary, but she couldn't help but overhear it.

"Yes, I remember. He's there already?" Ian glanced at his watch and was silent for a moment. "He's an hour early, but I can be there in fifteen minutes. OK. See you soon. Thanks."

He returned his phone to the holster on his belt and quickly drained the coffee from his cup. "Duty calls, I'm afraid. Jeff Andrews from the county economic development council is waiting in my office."

"I understand. Thank you for sharing your basket of goodies." Annie stood up and retied the plastic wrap around the basket. "Why don't you take the rest to the office so everyone can get a taste of what Takes the Cake has to offer? As much as I love sweets, I'll never eat all of this!"

Ian rose, collected their mugs and took them to the sink. "That's a great idea, if you're sure you won't eat them."

Annie patted her stomach and grinned. "There's no way I could—or should—polish off everything left in that basket. Spread the joy around your office." She handed the basket to him and led the way to the living room.

Standing at the front door, Annie put her hand on the doorknob and turned to face Ian. "This was a lovely way to start the day. Thank you."

He looked down and gazed into her eyes. Annie's hand shook on the doorknob. Would he kiss her again? She struggled to control her breathing.

"My pleasure. Definitely my pleasure." Ian stepped closer, one arm around the basket while the other reached out, his hand brushing a strand of hair from Annie's face.

He dropped his lips to hers and lightly kissed her. "I'm sorry I have to leave."

Annie, eyes locked with Ian's, absentmindedly opened the front door. "Me too."

She leaned on the open door and watched him take long strides down the path to the sleek black sedan waiting in the driveway. When the car disappeared from view, Annie closed the door. Leaning her back against it, she closed her eyes and drew in a deep breath, letting it trickle out her nose as she fought to slow her heartbeat. She stood there in a daze until a purring Boots, who had been curled up sleeping on the living room sofa all morning, rubbed against her legs.

Annie reached down and picked up the cat, cradling her in her arms. "Oh, Boots. Please tell me, am I wrong to have feelings for Ian?"

The feline looked up, her green eyes mirroring those of her adopted owner. All Boots could do was mew.

Annie stroked under Boots's chin. "I'll take that as a no. But why, then, do I feel so out of sorts?"

Rain began to pound the roof, and the old house creaked as the wind whirled against it. Annie carried Boots to the bay window in the living room and watched the angry sea crash against the rocks. "I suppose a walk on the beach is just not in the forecast today."

She placed an antsy Boots on the sofa and plopped down beside her to try to make sense of the thoughts zooming around in her head. Ian had kissed her, a tender but intense kiss. It was glorious. And terrifying. How can something feel so right and so wrong at the same time? A vision of Wayne

peering down from heaven and witnessing her kissing another man filled her with guilt. Closing her eyes, Annie did
the only thing she knew to do: pray.

First, Annie thanked God for sending Wayne to her and
for the wonderful years they had spent together. "He blessed
my life in so many ways, and I don't want to let go of these
memories," she whispered, the words barely audible above
the howling wind. "I am confused about my feelings for Ian.
I feel joy and guilt at the same time." Annie sat motionless
with her eyes closed as the house shuddered against the
wind, her thoughts whipping around in her head like tree
branches in the storm. How could she hear God speak if she
couldn't quiet her mind?

Taking slow, deep breaths, she recited the words from
Proverbs that always brought comfort during times of confusion. *"Trust in the Lord with all your heart, and lean not on
your own understanding; in all your ways acknowledge Him,
and He shall direct your paths."*

She repeated the verse until her heartbeat calmed and
her breathing became controlled. Her senses returning,
Annie reached for the notepad and pen sitting on the coffee table. She switched on the lamp next to her and neatly
wrote a to-do list: laundry, reply to emails from Texas, finish Ariel's sweater, and remove portraits from frames.

Moving through most of the day in a daze, Annie had
checked off the first three items and had fixed and consumed a dinner of fish and grits by six o'clock. Because grits,
a Southern staple, were hard to find in Maine, LeeAnn rou-
tinely mailed her a couple of boxes every few months. Annie
washed, dried, and put away her dinner dishes. The to-do

list, now hanging on the refrigerator amid colorful artwork by John and Joanna, reminded her of the last task: Remove portraits from frames.

Annie entered the library and stared at the portraits. Since the negatives hadn't turned up, perhaps Ian was right, and she should have the photographs digitally reproduced. But it just didn't seem right to use modern technology to restore historical photos. In a sense, it somehow seemed like cheating. Would a computer be able to do justice to the portraits?

Standing on her tiptoes, she grasped the bulky, ornate frame holding her grandparents' photo and lifted it from the wall. Crossing the room to the desk, she drew a tissue from the nearby box and dusted the back of the frame, sending a small cloud into the air. Her nose tickled as she turned over the frame to remove the photos. A sneeze welled inside her, and she grabbed a clean tissue. How long had it been since the portraits had been taken down from the wall?

Annie sat down and took a close look at the back of the frame. There was a rectangular pocket glued to the back. Holding the frame still with her left hand, she wriggled her right index finger into the narrow opening, wondering if she had found a letter or notes from her grandparents. Her finger pressed against a smooth plastic-like material. Sweeping the contents from the pockets with her fingertip, several strips of processed film slid onto the back of the frame.

Pulling the desk lamp closer, Annie turned the light to a higher setting and held a strip under the glow. She had found them!

She discovered a real treasure—a glimpse into the life

her grandparents had shared with her mother. Although the images on the black-and-white negatives were difficult to make out, she was pulled back in time by scenes of Grandpa fishing with a three- or four-year-old Judy, Gram sitting under a huge tree with what appeared to be her needlepoint, and apron-clad mother and daughter elbow-deep in a mixing bowl. Annie wished there were printed photos in the pocket so she could see the expressions on their faces. Her mind imagined happy, smiling countenances, and tears of joy spilled down her cheeks.

She pulled two business-size envelopes from a desk drawer and put the negatives in one of them. Hoping to find a similar pouch behind the family portrait, she retrieved the second frame from the wall and returned to the desk to find another glimpse into the past. The two top strips of negatives showed her mother, clad in what looked like a sailor dress, in different portrait poses. Annie held the third sheet to the light, surprised to find a young woman with long hair standing behind a large microphone stand. *Who is this?* Gram couldn't carry a tune in a bucket, so it wasn't her. The mystery singer filled each frame of the remaining three strips, but she couldn't see the pictures well enough to figure out where the photos had been taken.

Annie leaned back in the chair. *Who in the world is she?*

~ 6 ~

$\mathcal{T}$he final strains of the piano prelude were fading when Annie closed the large white door of Stony Point Community Church behind her and tiptoed into the last spot remaining in the back pew. As Reverend Wallace welcomed the congregation and recognized the morning's visitors, Annie glanced around to see if anyone had noticed her late arrival. She was relieved to find everyone focused on the bespectacled, portly pastor, his gray hair matching the weather outside, as he recited announcements from an index card. The tardiness of one of the church's most punctual members wasn't nearly as interesting as the plight of the Polk family.

"We all wait anxiously for warm sunshine and brighter days," the pastor said, "but we can spread cheer and hope by reaching out to little Matthew Polk with our prayers, kind words, and support of the upcoming fundraiser sponsored by the Stony Point High School student council here at the church community center. With our help and God's blessing, Matthew will have his eye surgery and will be back to riding his bicycle in no time."

Right on cue, Gloria Golden, the church's longtime pianist, lightly began the introduction to *Morning Has Broken*. Reverend Wallace motioned for the congregation to stand as folks lifted their hymnals.

Annie scanned the congregation in search of Ian. Most likely, he was sitting in his usual spot on the aisle in the fifth row, and she was grateful to have the wall of people between them. So far, she had been able to dodge his phone calls since "the kiss." But she couldn't avoid him forever.

Dropping her eyes to the songbook, Annie sang the last two lines of the second verse. "Praise for the sweetness of the wet garden, Sprung in completeness where His feet pass."

The words brought comfort she so deeply needed. Even if she didn't know what was happening with Ian, God did. The singing continued. "Praise with elation! Praise every morning, God's re-creation of the new day!"

The song ended and Reverend Wallace called the congregation's attention to the day's Bible verses, Psalm 139: 1–6 and 23–24.

"Read, listen, and find strength in God's Word," he said.

Annie opened her Bible to Psalm 139 and marked the page with her bulletin before taking a pencil from her purse. Pencil tip poised over the passage, she silently read along with the pastor, pausing from time to time to underline key words:

"O Lord, You have searched me and known me.
You know my sitting down and my rising up;
You understand my thoughts afar off.
You comprehend my path and my lying down,
And are acquainted with all my ways.
For there is not a word on my tongue,
But behold, O Lord, You know it altogether.

You have hedged me behind and before,
And laid Your hand upon me.
Such knowledge is too wonderful for me.
It is high; I cannot attain it."

The shepherd's words washed over Annie, and she silently prayed. *Lord, you understand my thoughts from afar. Please help me understand my own thoughts, my own actions. I love Wayne and miss him terribly. What do I do with these feelings for Ian?*

She drew a line under the last two verses in the passage.

"Search me, O God, and know my heart;
Try me and know my anxieties;
And see if there is any wicked way in me,
And lead me in the way everlasting."

Reverend Wallace closed his Bible and set it on the lectern. "Let us pray."

As the pastor started to lead the congregation in prayer, Annie silently mouthed one of her own. *Please, God, keep me from hurting Ian with my confusion. He is such a good man.* She tried to focus on the pastor's words of prayer, with varying degrees of success, and added her "amen" to the chorus of voices around her. As the service moved through the children's story, and then Reverend Wallace's message of hope and rejuvenation, Annie waivered in and out of conscious listening, often lost in her own thoughts. She was caught by surprise when Reverend Wallace's voice began the benediction.

"Now may the Lord of peace Himself give you peace, comfort, and hope, now and forevermore." He strode to the back of the church while Gloria, her head bobbing as her hands moved over the piano keys, filled the air with *This Is My Father's World.*

Annie stood with the congregation. She smiled and returned a wave to Josephine Booth, a library volunteer who had been childhood friends with Annie's mother, as she moved into the aisle and toward the door.

"Annie, how are you?" said a deep voice from behind her.

She turned to see Police Chief Reed Edwards standing next to her. "Good morning, Reed. I'm well, and you?" Annie hoped she seemed like her cheerful self, but she really didn't feel like it.

The chief lightly touched her forearm. "Everything has been quiet lately. I'm glad I've not made an official call to Grey Gables in quite some time. But it's good to see you in church."

"I agree, Reed, I agree." Annie inched closer to Reverend Wallace, who was standing by the door. "Stay safe out there now."

She glanced behind her and caught a glimpse of Ian and Alice deep in conversation while waiting to file out of the church. A pang of guilt shot through her. This was the first time in a long while she had not sat between them during Sunday services. *I should wait for them. But what would I say to Ian?*

Annie turned toward the door. Moving her Bible and church bulletin to her left hand, she held out her other hand to the pastor. "Good morning, Reverend Wallace. Your message was particularly appreciated today. Thank you."

"It's good to see you, as always, Annie." He held her hand a bit tighter and looked into her eyes. "Is everything all right? It's not like you to be late to church, even in the nasty weather we've been having lately."

* * * *

"Where have you been, and why aren't you answering your phone? Are you OK?"

Annie could hear Alice's lacquered nails tapping on the other end of the line. "I'm fine, Alice, really. I'm just trying to catch up on things around here. I've finished Ariel's sweater and boxed it for mailing and paid some bills."

Her friend's voice was tinged with concern. "Ian and I were worried about you Sunday. First you were late for church, and then you left without waiting for us. When you missed the Hook and Needle Club meeting this morning, I decided I was going to talk to you today if I had to hunt you down and hog-tie you to a chair!"

Annie walked from the kitchen into the living room, sat on the couch next to Boots, and wondered what to say to Alice, who knew her better than anyone except LeeAnn. "No hog-tying necessary, I'm sure. I'm sorry I worried you. Sometimes I still miss Wayne so much it overwhelms me. When I get like this it's better for me to ride it out by myself. I don't want to burden my friends."

Alice snorted. "Annie Dawson, that's about the silliest thing I've ever heard you say. A friend going through a tough time is not a burden. Your friends love you."

Annie rubbed the side of the cat's chin with her free

hand. "I'm blessed with good friends. That I know for sure. And I'm all right. I just have to work though these feelings."

"We missed you this morning. Vanessa updated us on the Polk family fundraiser. She's quite the event planner. Most of the arrangements are completed, including live entertainment, food vendors, and all sorts of sale items." Alice cleared her throat. "Vanessa asked how your rummage items and coasters were coming along. I didn't know what to tell her."

Guilt washed over Annie. The yarn and crochet needle remained unused in her craft bag on the end of the couch. "I'll start working on the coasters today; they won't take too long to complete once I get started."

A beep indicated an incoming call on Alice's phone. "Annie, this is a party hostess returning my call; I need to take this. But I'll call you tonight, OK? Just remember I'm right next door if you need me. Bye!"

"I'll be fine. We'll talk later. Bye." Annie switched off the phone and reached for her craft bag. "Well, Boots, I'd best get crackin' on these coasters."

Boots yawned, her eyes closing as she lowered her head back against the pillow featuring a Betsy Original cross-stitch of Butler's Lighthouse. Annie rose from the couch, crossed the room to the stereo, and tuned in to the classic rock station in Portland. *Maybe I'll crochet faster to rock music.*

Pulling out the pattern for the "Nature Star" coasters, her B hook, and the daffodil-color yarn from the bag, Annie started the first of six coasters in yellow. Her well-practiced fingers moved quickly, the hook grasped between the thumb and index finger of her right hand while the left hand worked the yarn.

Time slipped away into the music of the seventies, her fingers creating coaster after coaster as she sang along with bands from her high school years: The Eagles, Boston, Fleetwood Mac and Chicago. Before she knew it, six completed daffodil yellow coasters were stacked on the coffee table.

Tiring of the radio commercials, Annie put on one of her new jazz CDs before heading to the kitchen to fix a cup of tea. She returned to the living room with chamomile tea and a small bowl of mixed nuts. Taking a break from crocheting, she allowed herself to be swept away by the music.

Suddenly, tears begin dripping down her cheeks as she thought of Ian and her growing feelings for him. Guilt settled over her like the pervasive Maine fog. The house suddenly seemed confining, and a need to feel the cold wind and salt air overwhelmed her. She hurried to the mudroom, stepped into her boots, and put on her coat before following the path to the beach. The temperature was dropping as the afternoon faded. The wind stung her eyes, and the cold sent shivers down her spine. In a strange way, the discomfort began to clear away the fog in her head.

Do I love Ian? Is it really possible to love again? Mom and Dad died after sharing not only their love for each other but for God and mankind too. They didn't have a chance to grow old together. But Gram and Grandpa did. Gram's love for him never faded, even after he died. What is happening to my feelings for Wayne?

Memories of their years together flooded Annie's mind,

the little things that made life special—the smell of strong coffee brewing, televised Dallas Cowboy games, and holding hands in church. Even the way the twins tossed their heads when sudden happiness struck them reminded Annie of Wayne and the love they shared.

But dreams of Wayne are less frequent now, Annie thought. *Sometimes days pass without a thought of him. The hole in my life is still there. So why is the raw pain dimming?*

She closed her eyes and pictured Wayne at his desk in the Chevrolet dealership they ran together, eyes twinkling and lips smiling as she handed him a cup of coffee. *What if the pain fades to the point I can't remember him?* Annie shivered in the bitter wind. *Why did God give me this beautiful marriage, only to take Wayne before we grew old together like Gram and Grandpa? What am I to do with all of this life I have left?*

By the time she made her way back up the path to the house, the last signs of daylight were fading. The phone was ringing as she entered the house, but Annie climbed the stairs without answering it. Boots, sensing the change in Annie's demeanor, followed her upstairs for the night.

— 7 —

Standing on the edge of Town Square in Stony Point, Charlie scanned the crowd and contemplated joining a group of sailors gathered near the bandstand.

Then he saw her.

Charlie couldn't pull his gaze from the vivacious young woman as she dipped a ladleful of punch into a cup and handed it to her raven-haired younger sidekick. Keeping his eyes on her smile, he made his way through the growing crowd to the refreshment table.

"How's the punch?" Charlie smiled at the two friends and felt his face flush at their obvious delight at his presence.

"Delicious," the older girl said. She ladled punch into another cup and held it out to him. "Try some."

His hand tingled when his fingers brushed hers as he grabbed the cup. "Thank you, Miss ..." He hesitated, fighting the urge to brush a lock of her dark blond hair away from her green eyes.

"Betsy. And this is my friend, Stella. Nice to meet you."

Betsy placed a hand on Stella's arm as her young friend blushed and dropped into a slight curtsy. Charlie took a slow sip of the sweet, fruity liquid and tried to collect his thoughts. "I just came from nonstop noise in New York City. I like your Stony Point. It reminds me of home."

Betsy smiled. "Where is home?"

Charlie switched the cup to his left hand and wiped the other on his blue uniform trousers. "Connecticut. I was raised on a farm near Putnam. I'm on my way back home from the South Pacific by way of Los Angeles, Washington, D.C., and New York City."

Betsy reached for Charlie's empty cup, refilled it, and handed it back to him. "How did you end up in Stony Point?"

Grasping the proffered punch, Charlie nodded his thanks. "A buddy of mine left something behind on the ship. I stopped in Stony Point to give it to him. Maybe you know him—Harold Stevens?"

"Yes, we know Harold quite well," said Stella, tugging nervously on the skirt of her dress to smooth the navy blue fabric. "In fact, Betsy—"

Her words were interrupted by the arrival of Ethel Statom, Stella's piano teacher since childhood. "Stella, thank goodness I found you. The band is looking for someone to sing a song as a special tribute to the troops. I suggested you, of course. The bandleader is waiting for us by the bandstand."

Looking from Charlie to Betsy, Stella hesitated a moment before answering Mrs. Statom.

"I'd be honored," she said before turning to Charlie. "I hope to see you later. It was nice to meet you."

Charlie nodded. "My pleasure."

The pleasure, he thought, was having Betsy's undivided attention. They strolled around the park sharing bits about themselves. He learned she loved to cross-stitch, bake pies, and sit by the sea. She heard about the first time he saw a horse give birth, his habit of waking early enough to watch

the sunrise over the pasture, and the sense of satisfaction
he felt serving his country.

When the music began to play, Betsy and Charlie danced
an entire set, moving in sync as if they had been partners for
years. The music slowed, and they gazed into each other's
eyes as Stella's voice filtered over the dance floor.

"She has the most beautiful voice," said Betsy, glancing
at the stage. "She's usually so shy around people. I didn't
think they would get her onstage."

Charlie's eyes never left Betsy's face. "Yep."

The music stopped, and the bandleader stepped to the
microphone.

"Let's give the lovely young lady a round of applause ...."

*   *   *   *

Alice, her blue eyes flashing and right fist poised to resume frantic rapping on the door, jumped when it suddenly
swung open.

"Annie! Gosh, are you OK? My knuckles are bruised
from knocking so long. I was about to call Chief Edwards!
I've been trying to reach you since yesterday afternoon."

Annie blinked. "I don't even know when the phone rang
last. I'm all right. Come in, and I'll make some coffee." She
opened the door wider and ushered her friend into the living room.

Shrugging out of her jacket, Alice absentmindedly dis-
entangled her set of colorful bangle bracelets from her
sweater sleeve and then looked Annie in the eyes. "You don't
look OK to me. What gives?"

Annie hesitated and rubbed a hand over her face as her eyes filled with tears. "He kissed me."

Alice shook her head and raised her eyebrows as she hung her jacket on the coat rack. "Forgive me, but how is that a problem?"

"It's not funny." Annie's melodic voice was unusually tense. "I'm just really confused right now. I can't stop thinking about Wayne and how I'm being unfaithful to him. Tossing and turning all night did nothing to clear my head."

Alice opened her mouth to say tossing and turning did nothing to help her case of bed head, either. But Annie wasn't in the mood for teasing, so she exercised self-restraint. "This is huge, my friend. You know I'm here for you twenty-four seven, but you must face this head-on, and nobody is better suited to help you regain your footing than Reverend Wallace."

Stifling a yawn, Annie nodded. "Yes, you're right. Maybe I should give him a call."

Alice followed Annie to the kitchen as her concern mounted. The indecisive tone was unlike Annie. Her friend was known for sound judgment and an ability to focus on what needed to be done. The sleeping late, dark circles under her eyes, and slumped shoulders sounded alarm bells. Would she really make the phone call? Gently taking the bag of coffee from Annie's hands, Alice hugged her. "Annie, you look exhausted. Let me fix the coffee and call Reverend Wallace while you relax in a nice hot shower."

Stifling Annie's protest with a "shhh" and finger to her lips, Alice nodded to the doorway leading to the hallway and stairs. "Go. I'll make coffee." As soon as she heard Annie clear the stairs, she pulled out her cellphone and hit the church's speed-dial number. It didn't take long to get the minister on the line via his secretary, Ellen.

"Alice, how are you?" Alice instantly felt relieved when she heard Reverend Wallace's warm and jovial voice.

"I'm fine, Reverend, but I'm really concerned about Annie. She's going through a rough time right now, and I was hoping you would talk to her. She said it was all right for me to call you." Alice paused, unsure of how much to say. "She seems confused and listless. It's not like her. She's feeling a lot of guilt about Wayne."

Reverend Wallace sighed. "I'm tied up all day with the Stebbins family. Bill's funeral is this afternoon. Do you have time to stay with Annie most of the day to make sure she's all right? I can stop by Grey Gables first thing in the morning to see her."

"Sure thing," Alice said. "Anything for Annie. We can work on our needlecraft projects all day. Thanks for your help."

"You're very welcome. I'll see her tomorrow. And Alice, you did the right thing by calling me."

"I'm glad I did, Reverend. Please give my regards to the Stebbins clan. I was sorry to hear about Bill. Goodbye."

By the time Annie came downstairs looking more like herself in fresh clothes and makeup, Alice had not only fixed coffee, but had run to the carriage house and fetched homemade zucchini bread and her cross-stitch project for the rummage sale.

Pouring coffee into mugs, Alice gestured to the table, where a votive candle cast a warm glow over the bread and some of Annie's cream cheese, laid out artistically on

Betsy's good china. "Have a seat. I brought sustenance," Alice said. "I've been working almost nonstop this week, and I could use some quality girl time. We can yak to our hearts' content and maybe put a dent in our projects for the Polk family fundraiser. What do you think?"

Annie smiled as they pulled their chairs up to the table. "You are such a good friend. Thank you."

"Anytime. You'd do the same for me." Alice sipped her coffee. "Reverend Wallace will stop by to see you in the morning."

By the time the coffee and bread were nearly gone, Alice had heard enough stories about Wayne to love him for the happiness he had brought to her friend. He must have been something special for Annie's eyes to still sparkle when she spoke of him, especially in light of her apparent growing affection for Ian.

After tidying the kitchen, they settled on opposite ends of the sofa to work on their projects. Watching Annie create coaster after coaster with perfect, uniform stitches filled Alice with peace. Betsy would be proud of the woman her granddaughter had become. "Betsy is smiling down on us. You have her spirit, you know. She always said the best way to get out of a tough time is to *give* your way out. That's exactly what you do."

Annie reached out and fingered the coasters stacked on the coffee table. "Gram was a wise woman. I wish I had spent more time with her in her later years."

Placing her cross-stitch in her craft bag, Alice looked down the length of the sofa. "She understood you had your own life in Texas. But I'm glad she found a way to get you back to Stony Point."

"Me too." Annie jumped as the grandfather clock chimed two o'clock. "Wow, the time has passed quickly!"

Alice stood up, stretched her arms, and wiggled her fingers. "We're cooking with gas as far as the needlework projects go. Your stack of coasters is impressive, but you also promised Vanessa some rummage-sale items. Are you ready to tackle the attic after lunch? After all, what you need is another good mystery to occupy your mind. You've hit a dry spell."

A mischievous look flashed across Annie's face. "Well, not exactly a bone-dry spell."

Hands on her hips, Alice looked down at a grinning Annie. "Why, Annie Dawson, you've been holding out on me! You are going to tell me all about it as I fix us a salad—right?"

"No," Annie said as she rose to her feet. "I'll explain it as *we* fix the salad. And after we eat, we'll hit the attic."

By the time the shrimp and mixed-greens salad had been consumed, Annie had given Alice a blow-by-blow description of the quest for the negatives, including finding images of the mysterious singer. After they tidied the kitchen, Annie showed them to Alice.

Alice held a strip of negatives under the desk light in the library and let out a low whistle. "Old family photos, what a treasure! I just wish we could see the images better. Where's the mystery woman?"

Annie put another film strip up to the light. "Here is the singer. It's difficult to see her features. But it doesn't look like Gram."

Alice looked closer. "It's hard to tell. Maybe you should

take them to the next Hook and Needle Club meeting and show them to Stella. She might recognize her."

Switching off the light, Annie returned the negatives to the brown envelope and put them on the desk. "I'm not quite ready to share this mystery with anyone else yet. I want to have the photos printed first. Promise me you'll keep this to yourself for now."

"Oh, you're no fun," said Alice, giving Annie a light slap on the wrist. Remembering their pacts made when they shared secrets as kids, Alice held up the pinky of her right hand. "Oh, all right, spoilsport. I pinky promise."

Annie giggled and held up her own little finger. "Pinky promise."

Alice squeezed Annie's pinky with hers. "Pinky promise. Everything is going to be fine, better than fine. Now, let's go tackle that attic before we change our minds."

Following Annie upstairs to the attic, Alice was thankful to see her friend's spirits lifting. "Your attic is a mini-museum of Stony Point history. It's like the gift that keeps on giving with all of the rummage items you've found, family heirlooms discovered, and relatives located! And I, for one, am really thrilled with the track lighting you installed. It's not so spooky in here now."

Annie flipped a switch and the room filled with light. "I hope we can still find something worth selling at the fundraiser. I've cleared out a lot in the attic. But just when I think we've sorted through everything, we find something left untouched."

"Like this one?" Alice pushed against a trunk to reveal a low crawl space. "Did you bring a flashlight up with you?"

Annie pulled a mini-flashlight from her pocket and handed it to Alice before turning her attention to a nearby shelf. "I remember stashing a few trinkets over here when LeeAnn and I were up here playing dress-up with John and Joanna during their last visit. But feel free to crawl through the cobwebs if you want. I have a feeling you are about to enter the spooky zone."

Auburn head perched in front of the dark hole, Alice turned to look back at Annie. "Cover me, I'm going in!"

Annie looked up from the odd-shaped vase she held in her hand. "Go get 'em, Tiger!"

Alice, indeed, found plenty of cobwebs. Inching as far into the space as possible, she shined her flashlight along the sides to find several small storage boxes. The glint of metal caught her eye when the light hit the top of the box sitting at the farthest point in the space. Pulling her body forward, Alice reached her hand toward the sparkle until she finally grasped the box.

"Look what I found!" Alice said, after inching out of the crawl space. She raised the box in triumph. "Don't know what's in it, but the box sure is cool."

Annie set aside the rather abstract-shaped, pea-green vase and a set of sixties-era coasters she had found and stepped over to take the box from Alice. Wiping the dust off with her sleeve, Annie uncovered images of New York City landmarks. "This really is interesting. But my itchy nose is telling me to get out of the attic. Let's take the tin downstairs and open it in the library."

In short order they were sitting at Annie's grandfather's desk, studying the tin, which was about the size of the Bible the church gave to sixth-grade students at confirmation. Alice restrained herself from snatching it from Annie's hands. "Open it already. I'm about to burst with curiosity!"

Alice lowered her head closer to the tin as Annie pried off the lid. More negatives! She started to reach into the tin. "May I?"

Annie nodded. "Go for it!"

Lightly separating a sheet of film, Alice held it up to the desk light. "These are too dark to see very well, but the people look different from the negatives you found in the portrait. But they appear to be musicians at a microphone, just like your mystery singer."

Annie reached into the tin and pulled out an empty matchbook cover. "Ever heard of a club called The Avant-Garde? Look at this. Maybe it's a clue to the identity of these musicians."

Sitting back in her chair, Alice shook her head and held her out hand for the matchbook. Opening it flat, she looked to see if anything was written inside. It was blank. "Why do you think the negatives of the one singer were hidden in your family portrait instead of in the tin with this batch?"

"I haven't the slightest idea," Annie said, running an index finger along the rim of the tin and staring at its contents, "but I sure could use a cup of tea. Want some?"

Alice took the tin into the living room and put on one of Annie's new jazz CDs while Annie fixed tea in the kitchen. She couldn't take her eyes off the designs on the tin—the Empire State Building, the Statue of Liberty, the Brooklyn Bridge. *Who was the mystery singer, and why wasn't she in the tin?* Alice wondered.

Annie's voice cut into her thoughts. "Here we go. I took the liberty of fixing us a small snack." With a flourish, she placed a tray loaded with two cups of tea, cheese crisps, and apple slices on the coffee table.

Alice stirred cream and sugar into her tea. "I'm glad you're feeling better. I really was worried."

Silence filled the room. Annie drew in a long breath and slowly released it. "I guess I've been a bit self-centered lately. Ian's kiss threw me for a loop. You see, the way I responded to it scared me. I feel like I'm being unfaithful to Wayne."

Popping a cheese crisp into her mouth, Alice took time to consider her response. "Annie, although I never knew Wayne, I can feel his spirit through the memories you've shared of him. Someone who loved you that strongly would want you to be happy, even if it meant finding happiness with another man."

Adrift in her own thoughts, Annie's expression seemed a mixture of sadness and relief. Alice gently touched her arm. "Are you all right?"

Annie nodded. "Yes. It's just that Ian really is a good man, and I've hurt him by avoiding being alone with him lately. Do you think he has any idea how I feel about him?"

"I'm not sure you really know how you feel about him," said Alice. Not wanting to make light of the situation, she tried to stifle a laugh and the result sounded like a snort. "If he doesn't know you really, really like him, he's the only one in Stony Point who hasn't noticed!"

Blushing, Annie's eyes clouded. "Are people talking?"

"Relax," Alice said, taking a swig of tea. "I've tried to keep the gossip to a minimum."

Biting her lip, Annie sighed. "Alice, please don't talk about this with anyone. Ian and I need to see where this is going without any interference, even from friends with good intentions."

Chuckling softly, Alice realized just how well Annie had grown to know the good folks of Stony Point. "I promise to keep the town's worst-kept secret to myself. But the way you two look at each other tempts people to talk about it. You and Ian will have to go public sooner or later."

Annie brushed a stray hair from her eyes. "Yes, I know. Really, I do. I just want to feel comfortable with these feelings before I announce them to the world."

Glancing at the clock, Alice stood up. "It will be dark soon. I need to head back through the hedge. But I'll keep our conversation to myself." She held up her right pinky. "Pinky promise."

She was rewarded with Annie's lilting laugh.

"Pinky promise," Annie said, linking her pinky around Alice's finger.

— 8 —

Annie turned the well-worn book over to read the back cover. "Well, Reverend, it looks like I'm not the first to need the wisdom written in these pages."

Reverend Wallace adjusted his wire-framed glasses and pointed at the author's photo. "Wise man, Alan Negley. Always was, even when we were young men in seminary. He was giving relationship advice way back then. This was his first book, and it has come in handy over the decades."

The author-minister smiled up at her from the third edition of *Love, Loss, Life: Surviving the Loss of Your Soul Mate*. Like Reverend Wallace, he had a kind face and receding gray hair. Annie was beginning to feel better already. "Thank you for this and for your words of encouragement. They're just what I needed. I've not been quite myself lately; I don't understand it. Stony Point has become home. I have good friends here."

I really do have good friends here, friends who helped me work through the grief of losing Gram and the monumental job of sorting through her belongings, Annie thought. Yes, it had been tough being an outsider, even if she was Betsy Holden's granddaughter, but over time she had been accepted into the fold. Life was good.

"I don't understand why my emotions have been all over the board lately. I burst into tears over the most mundane things." Annie blinked back the tears starting to well in her eyes. "I am happy here. I treasure my friends. I love this house and its memories."

The minister took off his glasses, rubbing his eyes before returning the glasses to the bridge of his nose. "Annie, you do so much for others. You've taken strangers into your home, reunited friends with loved ones, and helped people heal after tragedy. But you've had a life-altering experience of your own with losing Betsy so soon after Wayne's death. And then you left your family in Texas and made a new home here. Now it's time to be good to *you*. All the feelings you've described to me are very normal."

Reverend Wallace took a deep breath and charged forward as if reading Annie's mind. "You know, Ian Butler is a good, solid man, and the two of you have grown closer lately. Could your friendship with him be causing these emotions you've described?"

Annie's eyes, wide with surprise, darted to his face. "Did Alice mention anything about Ian to you?"

The minister softly chuckled and put his hand over Annie's. "Alice didn't need to say anything. I've been watching a relationship develop between you and Ian for quite some time now. Your late entrance and hasty exit from church Sunday coupled with Alice's phone call about your emotional state were hints of your confusion."

Annie's eyes filled with tears. "Yes, I do have feelings for Ian. I've tried not to give in to them. They carry so many feelings of guilt. How can I care so much about Ian when I still love Wayne?"

Reverend Wallace tapped the book in Annie's hands.

"Read what my old friend says. Each chapter is coupled with Bible verses, so you can also read what God says about it. And I suggest you share your feelings with Ian. He's been through losing a spouse too. He'll most likely understand and have words of wisdom to share."

Annie nodded, clutching the book in her lap. "I think I'll read this first."

Reverend Wallace leaned forward to rise and spied the tin Alice had found in the attic. "What an unusual box," he said, nodding toward the tin on the coffee table. "It looks rather old. Did it belong to your grandmother?"

Annie picked up the box, holding it closer for him to see and lifted the lid, explaining her discovery of the negatives and the mystery of the singer. "I don't know where to get photos printed from negatives in this day and age of digital photography. But I am anxious to see what they contain."

He peered into the box and looked up. "Why don't you contact Ernst Michaels? He's a retired photojournalist in Petersgrove. He restored some old church photos for me several years ago. He's also a jazz buff. He might know something about your mystery singer. I have his number in my office. I'll call and give it to you later today."

Walking the minister to the door, Annie said, "Thanks for coming by. You've been a great help."

Reverend Wallace paused on his way out the door. "Annie, please don't spend too much time alone. And remember, you have a lot of people in Stony Point who care about you. Keep in touch."

*   *   *   *

"So, did you call the photographer?" Alice called soon after Annie had hung up the phone with Ernst Michaels.

"Yes, ma'am, I sure did." Annie put on her reading glasses and looked at the directions sitting on top of the tin where it still rested on the coffee table. "He is expecting me—er, us—at three o'clock. You do want to go with me, right?"

"Wouldn't miss it for the world! What time should I pick you up?"

Annie looked at the bags of coasters on the coffee table surrounding the tin. "Well, I'd like to stop by A Stitch in Time on the way to get more yarn to make matching place mats to go with the coaster sets. It will take a while to get to Petersgrove, so about one o'clock? But it's my turn to drive."

*   *   *   *

Mary Beth growled and slammed down the phone receiver just as Annie and Alice walked into A Stitch in Time. "Thanks for nothing!"

Alice looked at Annie. "Was it something we said? Maybe we need to go out and come in again."

Mary Beth looked up from the checkout counter. "I'm so sorry; that definitely wasn't intended for you." She waved her hands toward the back of the store. "All the rain we've had lately was too much for the roof. Leaks are springing up all over the place, some producing drips and others rivers. I've been calling roofing companies since early this morning. I just can't seem to get anyone out here to fix it—Mother Nature has created some brisk business for roofers. But that isn't your problem. What can I do for you ladies?"

Annie looked at the water puddle along the rear wall. "Oh, Mary Beth, what a mess! It looks like we came at a bad time. Can we help stack things away from the water? Maybe we can move some of your inventory to Grey Gables. Or maybe it would be better if we just come back tomorrow."

Shaking her head, Mary Beth came out from behind the counter. "Please stay. I can't seem to do anything about the water situation right now anyway, and Kate will be in soon to help with the damage control. What can I do for you?"

Annie held up a pattern for a place mat similar to the coasters, only larger. "Is there a multicolored cotton yarn that would match close enough to all of the different colors I used for the coasters?"

Mary Beth led her to a bin of multicolored yarns of varying hues as Alice went to check out the puddles of water growing in size and number.

Alice stuck the toe of one shoe up to the waterline in the back corner of the building and looked at the soggy boxes stacked nearby. "Wow, this *is* a mess! I hope insurance covers the cleanup."

Holding up several skeins for Annie to see, Mary Beth sighed loudly. "I can't believe the timing. I'm scheduled to leave Thursday for the National Fiber Arts Convention in New York City next weekend. I paid for it months ago. I even made arrangements for my niece to mind the shop so Kate could go."

From her purse, Annie pulled sample pieces of the yarn used for the coasters and held them up to the skeins in Mary Beth's hands. After considering all of them, she made a choice. "I'll take several of this one. And maybe the water mess will be all cleaned up by next week, and you'll still be able to attend the conference."

A loud groan filtered through the shop as Alice discovered more leaks. "I don't see how she can unless a band of elves magically cleans up all this for her. I wouldn't even know where to start!"

Mary Beth began ringing up Annie's purchase. "Alice is right. There's no way to handle this and prepare for the trip." She placed the yarn in a bag. "Hmm, would you two be interested in going in my place? Kate is going too. You can have a girls' weekend in the city and bring back ideas for the shop and the club."

Annie and Alice exchanged meaningful looks as Mary Beth scanned Annie's debit card. "Can you say 'road trip'?" Alice rubbed her hands together in anticipation, her bracelets jingling.

Annie's left elbow connected with Alice's right side. "Can we let you know in a day or two? I need to see if I can reschedule a few things." She took the card back from Mary Beth. "But the conference sounds fun."

Mary Beth handed the yarn-filled bag over the counter. "Sure thing. Is it all right if I tell Kate she might have company in New York? Right now she is concerned about hitting the Big Apple alone."

"Absolutely. I hope it works out for us to pinch-hit for you." Annie moved toward the door. "Good luck with the water cleanup!"

Minutes later, Annie and Alice were settled in Annie's car, listening to classic rock music and discussing the possibility of a trip to New York as they drove to Petersgrove.

Alice turned down the music. "Annie, we have to go to New York. It's our opportunity to find The Avant-Garde! We might be able to find out the identity of the mystery singer and her connection with your grandparents. Just what do you have to do that is so important?"

The wind whipped around the car, and Annie steadied the steering wheel. "Nothing too dire. I just wanted to make sure Mary Beth was thinking it through and not just reacting to the emergency. We didn't really have time to explain about the singer and the photo negatives. And keep in mind, Master Sleuth Woman, that if we decide to attend the conference, we're doing it to help Mary Beth, not to go off on our own little adventures. The conference will come first."

Alice sighed. "You always were the responsible one."

"Well, someone had to be!" Annie laughed, enjoying the lighthearted moment.

The ride passed quickly as the two friends swapped memories and banter. They were surprised when the quaint wooden "Welcome to Petersgrove" sign appeared. Ernst Michaels's home, a charming beige cottage with blue-gray shutters and surrounded by a white picket fence, was located on the far edge of the small town.

"This is it," said Alice, double-checking the house number on the directions. "He must be married. This is way too cute to be the abode of a jaded photojournalist."

Laughing, Annie reached to the passenger-side floorboard for the canvas bag resting against Alice's legs and removed the small envelope containing the photo negatives and a larger one with the two portraits. "Here we go! I sure hope he can help us. He said his studio is at the back of the house."

Annie knocked on the studio door with anticipation, a welcome change to her volatile emotions of the last couple of weeks. Although she had no preconceived notions of what a photojournalist might look like, she was surprised when the door opened to reveal a thin greyhound of a man wearing faded blue jeans and clogs, his balding salt-and-pepper hair trimmed close to his head.

"You must be Annie Dawson." He opened the door for them to enter. "Ernst Michaels." He grasped Annie's hand in a firm handshake before turning to Alice. "And you are?"

Alice held out her hand. "Alice MacFarlane, sidekick sleuth."

Mr. Michaels grinned. "I see. I must admit I'm intrigued. Being somewhat of a music-history buff myself, I'm anxious to see what you have here."

Annie handed him the envelope with the film negatives. "We are too. Thank you for seeing us so quickly."

Crossing the room to a long work counter, Mr. Michaels switched on a lighted slide viewer and placed a strip of negatives on it. "These are in pretty good shape, especially for being in an attic for decades. I can get some pretty good prints from them."

Alice stepped closer to see the images on the viewer and squinted. "How on earth can you tell?"

Mr. Michaels's laughter was deep and melodic. "Decades of working with film. Not many of us do that anymore."

"You're telling me." Annie leaned over to see the negatives. "Oh, I nearly forgot the reason I contacted you in the first place!" She took the two portraits from their envelope and handed them to the photographer. "These are the portraits I'd like reprinted. If printing from the negatives works best, that's fine with me, but I thought I'd leave these in case the others don't process well."

He studied the portraits a minute. "I'll try to work with the negatives first. The printed portraits have faded over the years. If necessary, I can scan them and do touch-ups digitally. I'll call you when they're ready. It should only take a couple of days. You caught me during a slow week."

Taking one last peek at the negatives, Annie lifted both her purse and canvas bag to her shoulder and held out her right hand. "That works for me. Thank you so much."

*   *   *   *

Ernst Michaels stood at the door and watched the two women walk the path from his studio toward their car. When they disappeared into the front yard, he returned to the viewer and studied the images. Was his imagination playing tricks on him? He blinked his eyes and looked more closely. "You've got to be kidding me—it can't be!"

After several long minutes, the photojournalist pulled his cellphone from its holster and quickly dialed. "It's Ernst. You're not going to believe what I'm looking at right now!"

— 9 —

nnie and Alice stepped out of the church into breezy sunshine and a group of folks milling around, discussing Reverend Wallace's sermon and news from the week.

"You look great, Annie! Better than I've seen in days." Alice put her lips to Annie's ear. "Having a mystery to solve agrees with you!"

Before Annie could reply, her cellphone vibrated in her purse. "Hello? Yes, this is Annie. Yes. I can be there in about an hour. Thank you. I'll see you then. Bye!"

"Was that Mr. Michaels?" Alice moved closer again. "Any news?"

Annie nodded. "The prints are done. He sounded really excited. Ready for a return trip to the big metropolis of Petersgrove?"

Ian approached before Alice could reply. "Heading out for a drive, are you?"

Seeing Ian, Annie's stomach churned as her heart swelled. "Yes, we're going to pick up the prints for the portraits."

Looking at her watch, Alice sighed. "I just remembered I need to contact clients to reschedule my Thursday and Friday Divine Décor and Princessa jewelry parties to clear the way for our New York trip."

Ian glanced from Alice to Annie. "New York?"

"Ian, why don't you go to Petersgrove with Annie, and she can tell you all about the trip and her new mystery." Alice grinned, her eyes shining in triumph. "Then I won't feel so guilty about bailing out on her. Besides, you always enjoy helping out with Annie's mysteries."

Annie tried to read Ian's expression. Did he really want to go? And was she ready to be alone with him again? "I'd love for you to fill in for Alice, if you have time." She tried to control her breathing. Was that a sparkle in his eye?

Taking his cellphone from its holder, Ian punched several numbers. "No messages. I'm clear for the afternoon if you'd like some company. I'll drive if you like, and you can leave your car at Grey Gables."

Pulling car keys from her purse, Alice prepared to leave. "I'd best get going now. Please call me when you get the photos, OK?" She gave Annie a quick hug and almost danced down the sidewalk.

*　*　*　*

"So, tell me about this trip to New York." Ian kept his eyes on the road to Petersgrove as he passed a logging truck.

Annie recounted her last visit to A Stitch in Time, the flooded building, and Mary Beth's request that Alice and Annie accompany Kate to the fiber arts convention in her place.

"I've never been to New York City, although I've been to a number of other big cities like Dallas, Detroit, and Atlanta. I was never interested in visiting New York until last week, when I came across some old photos of Grandpa taken there after he returned from World War II. Now I feel some sort of a connection." Annie studied the angle of Ian's jawline. His strong good looks were difficult to ignore.

Ian glanced at her before returning his eyes to the road. "Everyone should experience New York City at least once in their lives. It has creative electricity not found anywhere else. The city was good to me after Arianna died. Its vibrancy helped me heal."

Unsure of how to respond to his reference to his late wife, Annie fell silent for a few minutes and watched the scenery change from farmland to woodland. "Well, there's another reason for me to go to New York."

"It wouldn't have anything to do with the mystery Alice mentioned, would it?"

Was that amusement in his voice? Annie giggled. "As a matter of fact, it does." She explained her discovery of the mystery singer's image behind her grandparents' portraits and elicited laughter from Ian with her humorous description of Alice's adventure among the cobwebs in the crawl space.

"I would have paid good money to see that," he said, chuckling. "So, what was in the tin box she found?"

He listened quietly as Annie told him about the photo negatives of musicians, the matchbook cover, and the excitement in the photographer's voice during the phone call earlier. "Annie, I haven't been to the Big Apple for several years, but The Avant-Garde was still open when I was there. I don't remember the address, but I did see a couple of shows at the club. It has a long history of drawing in jazz greats to perform."

Annie caught her breath. "It's still there? Really?"

Ian reached across the car and put his hand on hers. "Annie, you have to go to the conference. It's the perfect opportunity to learn more about the club and maybe learn the identity of the mystery singer, not to mention that you will be helping out Mary Beth."

She squeezed his hand. "I see the logic in that, but what will I do about Boots? I can't just leave her."

Ian thought a minute. "How about Breck? He's demonstrated an ability to accept responsibility at the diner. He's doing some serving now as well as busing tables. And he likes you. I bet he'd do it."

Annie thought of the lanky, long-haired high school dropout who had recently returned to night school to earn his diploma. He'd really come out of his shell since taking the busboy job at The Cup & Saucer. Peggy talked like he might soon be promoted to server. "That's an idea! He's such a great kid, and he's come so far. I'll stop by the diner tomorrow and see if he would take care of Boots for me."

By the time Ian pulled in front of Ernst Michaels's home and studio, Annie had decided to take the trip to New York City. "Let's hope Mr. Michaels has some answers for us."

Filled with anticipation, Annie knocked on the studio door. After Annie introduced the two men, Mr. Michaels quickly led his visitors inside and motioned them to his work table. A series of black-and-white photos of various jazz musicians in a smoke-filled, haunting nightclub spread from one end to the other.

Ian let out a long, low whistle. "Look at this—there's everyone from Ella Fitzgerald and Duke Ellington to Stan Getz and Artie Shaw."

Annie's eyes went straight to a stunning blonde with fingers curved around an old-fashioned microphone as tendrils of cigarette smoke curled around her. Speechless, Annie looked at Mr. Michaels, who was obviously enjoying their reactions to the photographs.

"You are looking at photographs by one of the best photojournalists of all time, the award-winning Leo Harmon. The few photos this artistic genius took during the Jazz Era in New York City are iconic and included in everything from textbooks to coffee-table books as well as private art and museum collections all over the world." Mr. Michaels looked like a little kid surveying his new toys on Christmas morning. "You, Annie Dawson, have solved one of photography's oldest mysteries: What happened to Harmon's lost jazz negatives?"

Annie kept looking at the blond singer. "We may have solved one mystery, but we sure do have a lot more questions. How did Leo Harmon's negatives get in my attic? Who is the blonde, an unknown among all the jazz greats? And why were the negatives of her photos behind my grandparents' portrait?"

Michaels gathered up the photos and divided them into several brown-paper sleeves. "I don't know. But you'll want to keep the negatives in a safe or a safety deposit box at your bank. They will be in demand once word gets out that you have them." He handed her the paper sleeves and a smaller envelope containing the negatives.

Michaels gestured to four 11 by 14-inch photos on his drafting table. He'd restored each of the two family portraits two ways—one as an enlarged traditional reprint and the other as a digital copy. "These appear to be Harmon's too. But I never heard about him taking family portraits. His work was usually for newspapers or magazines."

He slid the portraits into a large brown sleeve. "I put the negatives in the envelope with the jazz series." Michaels walked to his desk and returned with the New York–themed tin. "This is probably worth some money too."

Handing the photos and tin to Ian, Annie wrote a check for the retired photojournalist's work. "Thank you so much, Mr. Michaels. You've been a big help."

Mr. Michaels shook Annie's proffered hand. "Anytime. I'm glad you found me. Please let me know if you solve your mystery."

*   *   *   *

Annie and Ian walked onto the porch of Grey Gables hand in hand.

"Thank you for putting the negatives in the safe at Town Hall until I can get to the bank." Annie put her key in the front door. "Will you join me for a cup of tea?"

Their eyes locked. Annie caught her breath and thought she would drown in his chocolate brown eyes before he answered.

"Sure! I've not seen nearly enough of you lately." Ian opened the door and stepped aside. "And you may keep the negatives in the safe as long as necessary."

Annie hung their coats on the rack. "Make yourself comfortable on the couch. I'll fix refreshments and will be right back."

She returned shortly with a tray bearing a full teapot, two mugs, and a small plate of cream cheese and pepper jelly surrounded by crackers. "Here we go, a bit of sustenance to end an exciting afternoon." After filling each mug, she handed one to Ian, following his gaze to Reverend Wallace's book.

Ian cleared his throat and looked at her. "Annie, do you have reservations about our friendship?"

Annie's hand trembled as she grasped her mug. She chose her words with care. "I've been feeling guilty about my feelings for you. When you kissed me, I felt like I was cheating on Wayne. I never expected to have feelings for anyone else." She reached out for the book. "Evidently, I'm pretty transparent. Reverend Wallace offered me this book to read. He also told me to talk to you."

"Well, I do understand what it is like to lose your soul mate. Moving on feels like infidelity, although it isn't. It's taken me time to understand this, but your Wayne and my Arianna would want us to find happiness again." He tapped the book in Annie's lap. "By the way, Reverend Wallace gave me this same book to read several years ago. A lot of wisdom can be found in those pages."

Boots wandered into the room, jumped onto the couch between them, and curled into a ball. Annie gently scratched under the cat's chin with two fingers. "The book helps. So does Reverend Wallace's guidance. Even Boots provides comfort. But I don't understand the feelings I have right now, and I'm just not ready to define them."

Ian put his mug on the coffee table and looked into her eyes. "Annie, I won't push you to define those feelings until you are ready. We have no reason to rush into anything."

Relieved but unsure of what to say next, Annie spread a bit of cream cheese on a cracker and put it in her mouth. By the time she swallowed the bite, her composure was regained. "Thank you."

Reverting to their normal banter, they finished their tea and crackers. By the time Annie walked Ian to the door, she had promised him she would accompany Alice and Kate to New York and share her mystery with the Hook and Needle Club on Tuesday. "Thank you for today," Annie said as she turned the doorknob.

Ian bent down and kissed Annie's cheek. "Thank you for including me. And I'm glad we had a chance to talk. Good night."

"Good night." Annie stood at the door and watched Ian turn and walk across the porch. "Ian." Annie's heart skipped when he turned around, a questioning expression on his face. She closed the distance between them and tiptoed to lightly press her lips to his. "Thank you for being patient."

Without waiting for a response, she turned and went inside the house.

~ 10 ~

Annie stepped inside A Stitch in Time, and her jaw dropped. The shop looked better than it had a few days ago—the water puddles were gone and fewer boxes were stacked in the middle of the floor—but buckets remained in several strategic spots in the event of more rainfall before the roof was repaired. A musty smell filled the shop. Mary Beth obviously had a long way to go before the shop was back to normal.

"Oh, Mary Beth. We should've cancelled the meeting. I had no idea the shop was in this condition."

The shopkeeper maneuvered around a short stack of boxes as she waved. "I considered it. But Kate convinced me that seeing my friends would relieve my stress a bit and force me to take a break from the mess."

Alice emerged from between lines of shelves carrying a load of boxes and put them down near the cash register. "Hi, you! I came early to help Mary Beth clear a space to work." She turned to her friend. "I know it must seem like a losing battle, Mary Beth, but I think Annie has some news that might cheer you up."

Mary Beth wiped sweat off her forehead with the back of her hand, leaving her short gray hair matted. "Can you believe I've worked up a sweat when it is still so blustery outside?" She looked from Alice to Annie. "So, what's your news?"

Annie made a funny face at Alice. "Don't you think we should wait until everyone else arrives before we share?"

"Spoilsport," Alice replied, mimicking Annie's expression.

"You two are hysterical," Mary Beth said with a smile, her mood seeming to brighten a little. "Well, Kate is in the storeroom, and Stella is homebound with a cold. Jason called and said she didn't want to spread her germs around the group. So we are just waiting on Gwen and Peggy. I shouldn't have to wait long to hear your news." She leaned against the counter and glanced around, grimacing at the scene. "Suppose we could fit six chairs here in this open area near the register?"

By the time Gwen arrived and Peggy came breezing in, breathless after sprinting from next door, Annie and Alice had arranged their normal cluster of chairs in a dry area surrounded by stacks of relocated stock. They took their seats when Kate returned from the storeroom.

"Vanessa asked me to give you an update on the fundraiser. It's scheduled from 11 a.m. to 4 p.m. two weeks from Saturday at the community center. They've booked a number of entertainment acts, from magicians and balloon artists to school musicians and community groups," said Kate, sitting in her chair with a steno pad of notes on her lap and a pen in her hand. "She asked me to make a list of what the Hook and Needle Club will be selling."

Gwen pulled a pink-and-lavender work-in-progress from the canvas bag at her feet. "I found a pattern for this adorable cellphone cozy online. Can't you see a teenage girl grabbing one of these? I hope to get several made by the day of the event."

Peggy held up her nearly finished Noah's Ark baby quilt, the colorful zoo animals eliciting oohs and aahs from her friends. "Isn't this sweet? I should have it done by our next meeting."

Looking around the room, Kate shook her head. "I've not had time to think about it since we had our own personal flood in the shop. I thought for a while there that *we* should be building an ark. Then there's the National Fiber Arts Convention this week. But I have half a dozen reusable shopping bags I crocheted earlier this year. I can donate those to the cause."

"I have a dozen cross-stitch bookmarks of varying designs," said Alice, pulling a fistful from her bag. "I thought we might pair each with a donated book."

When it was Mary Beth's turn to speak, she shrugged her shoulders. "The roof leak derailed my plans. I don't know if I'll pull it together fast enough to finish anything or not, but maybe I can find something in the shop to offer at our table. She paused, closing her eyes in concentration. "Oh, when Jason called to tell me Stella was homebound, he said she was knitting a herringbone belt for the fundraiser."

Alice cleared her throat, her eyes twinkling. "Annie has place mats and coasters." She paused, allowing a dramatic silence to fill the air before she continued. "And she has a new mystery!"

Hands on hips, Peggy adopted her best aggravated parent look. "A new mystery and you've waited this long to tell us!"

All eyes were on Annie as she removed the photographs and matchbook cover from her bag. "It all started when I decided to have the portraits of Gram, Grandpa, and Mom restored."

Annie described the search for the negatives and her discovery of them on the backs of the frames. One by one, she held up the prints of her mother and grandparents so everyone could see. "In the middle of the negatives for these photos, I found this." She passed around the image of the singer so everyone could see it.

"She's beautiful! Who is she?" Peggy was sitting on the edge of her seat. "Do you know where this was taken?"

Alice gently took the matchbook from Annie's fingers. "This is where I come in. Bear with me as I set the stage." Using her hands to describe her discovery of the crawl space and old tin, she finally revealed it held old photo negatives of jazz musicians, the likes of Ella Fitzgerald, Charlie Parker, and Tommy Dorsey. "This empty matchbook from a New York jazz club was in there too. We assume the blonde was a jazz singer since she was in with all of the others, but no one recognizes her."

The matchbook was also passed around in a grown-up version of the grade-school favorite, show-and-tell. Gwen, who enjoyed weekend shopping trips to New York City, rubbed her neatly manicured fingers over the front of the cover. "It's a long shot, but do you suppose the club is still there?"

A mock coughing sound blurted from the other side of the circle. "Good point, Gwen!" Mary Beth was grinning. "Sounds like a great reason for Annie and Alice to take my place at the conference. You can craft during the day and sleuth at night."

Peggy plucked the matchbook from Gwen's hand, maneuvering it around her long, curved acrylic fingernails. "Annie, she's right, this is the perfect opportunity for you to look into whether or not the jazz club still exists and see if anyone knows anything about the unknown singer, not to mention how the tin of negatives landed in your attic."

Annie looked at Kate. "What do you think?"

Kate waved the photos that had made their way around the circle to her. "I think I'm happy to have two friends going to explore New York with me! Do you want me to drive since I have a van?"

Annie and Alice quickly agreed.

"Great!" Kate said. "I'll pick you both up around eight o'clock Thursday morning."

The issue settled, the group dispersed, with Peggy and Annie walking next door to the diner—Peggy to return to her shift and Annie to ask Breck about taking care of Boots.

"I'm going to have a quick chicken salad sandwich," Annie told Peggy before heading to a booth. "Would you send Breck over to see me when he has a spare minute?"

*   *   *   *

Annie was filled with satisfaction Wednesday afternoon as she checked off another item on her to-do list and looked at the old grandfather clock. With Breck due to arrive any minute to meet Boots and pick up the house key, little was left for her to do. She had already called to stop the newspaper delivery for the rest of the week, finished most of her packing, and called Chief Edwards to request a special patrol drive-by for the house while she was gone. Even Ariel's pooch sweater was en route to Texas!

And she had a surprise for Alice and Kate. A quick computer search had brought good news: Ian was right. The Avant-Garde was still open and very much a hot spot for jazz!

The doorbell rang just as the clock began to chime the six o'clock hour. Boots wandered into the living room when Annie opened the door for Breck to enter.

"Hi, Breck. Welcome to Grey Gables." Annie scooped the cat into her arms. "And this is Boots. She pretty much rules the roost, or at least she thinks she does!"

The gangly teen scratched the cat's head. "Hi, Boots." He looked up at Annie. "Hi, Mrs. Dawson. Cool cat."

Closing the door, Annie released a purring Boots, who kept Breck immobilized while making figure eights around his legs. "She likes you already! And Boots is a really good judge of character."

Annie motioned Breck toward the kitchen. "Her food and water bowls are in the kitchen, near the mudroom door."

After demonstrating the correct proportion of dry to canned cat food for each meal, Annie gave him a copy of the house key. "Sometimes I let Boots roam outside, but it's been so cold that I think you should keep her inside. She has the run of the house. Just check her food and water each day."

Annie showed Breck where to find the cat litter and scoop under the sink. "Please check the litter box and clean it out if necessary," she said. "You shouldn't need to change the litter unless Boots goes wild and empties it onto the floor."

Breck stared at the litter box with raised eyebrows. "Does that happen often?"

Laughing, Annie gave him a reassuring pat on the arm. "Don't worry, she's pretty neat."

They crossed the hall to the library. "I cancelled the newspaper delivery for the rest of the week. But if the deliveryman leaves one anyway, just put it on the desk in here with the mail. That's about it, but I do want to warn you about the front door."

Annie explained the old lock and how easy it was to get locked out of the house if the mechanism on the door edge just below the deadbolt was depressed. "The deadbolt key won't help you if this happens. Just make sure you don't accidently press this button. When you close the door, give it a bit of an upward pull so it will close all the way."

Breck nodded. "I understand. We have an old house too."

Annie watched with satisfaction as Breck knelt to rub underneath the cat's chin, causing the purring to grow louder and the furry gray head to tilt back to one side. "I think the two of you will get along famously."

*　*　*　*

The first flickers of daylight cast odd shadows along the bedroom wall when Annie woke to find Boots curled up near the pillow, gently flicking the tip of her tail as a wake-up call. "Good morning. You're up early." She rubbed her eyes and stared at the clock. It wasn't even six thirty yet. "You know something's going on, don't you?"

A white paw lightly reached out and nudged Annie's

cheek in response. She rubbed a hand down the cat's back from neck to tail. "You are such a comfort, Boots. Whatever would I do without you?"

At six thirty, Annie stretched, crossed the cold floor to don her robe, and wandered downstairs to start a pot of coffee so it would be brewing while she showered. It was useless to try to sleep any longer when she was just hours away from experiencing the excitement of The Big Apple and possibly discovering clues to the mystery singer's identity! By the time Kate and Alice drove up in Kate's minivan, Annie's suitcase, craft bag, and a large insulated carafe of coffee and three travel mugs in a small canvas bag were already sitting by the front door of Grey Gables.

"Good morning!" Annie threw open the door as Alice and Kate stepped onto the front porch. "I'm all ready. I just want to leave a quick note for Breck and say goodbye to Boots."

Alice still looked sleepy. "Is that coffee?" she asked, peeking into the bag. "Bless you! I'll grab your bags if you'll share your coffee."

Annie snickered. Alice must have been half asleep if she didn't notice the three mugs by the carafe. "Grab away. I'll just be a minute! Kate, please make sure Alice doesn't run into anything before I get back out here."

Taking quick, long steps through the house, Annie double-checked the cat's water and food bowls before jotting a quick thank-you note to Breck. On her way back to the front door, she made sure timers were set on the lamps by two of the living room windows. Just before leaving, she bent down to give Boots a rub before walking onto the front porch. "Be good, Boots. I'll see you Sunday!"

"Get a load of that spaghetti bowl!" Alice cast aside her cross-stitch, eyes bouncing from the endless line of slow-moving traffic to the massive knot of roads at the Interstate 95 interchange in New York City.

Kate's knuckles turned white on the van's steering wheel as she took a deep breath and tried to focus on the traffic in front of her. "I've never seen anything like it. Sort of makes Hartford look like a hole in the wall, doesn't it?" Her voice was soft, the words lifting slowly into the air. Her heart was thumping so fast she wondered if her friends could hear it. "It might take longer to travel the last twelve miles than it did the rest of the trip combined."

Annie, sitting in the passenger side backseat, leaned as far forward as her shoulder strap would allow. "Not even all the automobile trade shows Wayne and I attended in Detroit prepared me for this." She looked at her watch. Three o'clock. "I read a blog suggesting travelers get through this spot by three o'clock because it becomes gridlocked during rush hour. Man, they weren't kidding!"

Tapping her fingertips on the steering wheel, Kate searched for a balance between staying alert and remaining calm. She risked a glance in the rearview mirror. "Annie, did you and Wayne go on a lot of business-related trips?"

Distracted for a moment as a dilapidated old brown

station wagon crawled alongside the van, Annie watched the young woman driver talk on a cellphone while two toddlers sat side by side in car seats in the back. "We went to Detroit each year and attended a state association convention annually, but mostly we networked with the local chamber of commerce."

Kate sighed. "You two must have spent a lot of time together." What would it be like to have a real partnership with a man who loved and respected her? Harry was too busy battling his own demons—drinking and self-doubt—to be a partner with any woman. The divorce had been both painful and a relief. "I miss having a man in my life. I stayed in touch with that detective we met in Texas, but it's hard to keep a long-distance relationship going. Oh well, I've grown to value my independence. Still, it would be nice to have the love of a good man."

Alice cringed next to her and pressed an imaginary brake pedal with her right foot, and Kate wondered if her friend was reacting to the conversation or the shiny yellow sports car cutting in front of the van.

"Oh, I don't know. I enjoy having a man to accompany me to concerts, movies, and the occasional dinner, but mostly I like making my own decisions," Alice said, releasing her foot from the floorboard.

Traffic picked up more speed, and Kate looked for a sign indicating how far they were from the downtown exit. She'd feel better if she knew where she was going. As if reading her mind, Alice began punching keys on her cellphone GPS, and soon, with Alice's help, Kate was navigating the van through the spaghetti bowl. "We have two exits coming up quickly."

Before long, Kate was getting a crash course in driving among urban maniacs in Midtown Manhattan. She winced as a taxi careened around a corner in front of her and slid to a stop in front of a swanky-looking bistro. "Toto, I've a feeling we're not in Stony Point anymore."

Annie's eyes followed the harried taxi patron dashing from the vehicle to the restaurant. "I have to tell you, Kate, I'm so glad you are the one driving on this trip!"

Kate smiled for the first time since approaching the city. "I must admit I'm happy Mary Beth splurged on the on-site parking. I'm prepared to learn the ins and outs of taxi and subway travel for the duration of our stay."

Alice let out a long, low whistle and pointed to a towering glass-and-steel building just ahead. "And that, ladies, is our humble abode for the next three nights."

The sound of Annie's humming filtered from the backseat as Kate pulled the van up to the valet parking stand. Before the parking attendant reached for the door handle, the three friends broke into song, "It's up to you, New York, New York!" The trio retrieved their luggage from the back of the van during the final chorus.

Laughing with relief, Kate accepted the claim ticket from the tuxedo-clad attendant. "I've never been so glad to see my vehicle driven by someone else!" she said, watching the van disappear into the parking area.

Annie placed a hand on Kate's shoulder. "Really? You seemed as cool as a cucumber. I never would have guessed you were stressed. Impressive."

Following the bellboy to the polished marble front desk, they looked around in awe while waiting to check in. Large glass elevators zoomed visitors up what seemed like forty floors or more. Gift shops and restaurants were tucked among large indoor gardens and fountains, and a large marquee listed various events currently held in the convention center.

"Mary Beth really splurged on this convention. What a shame she can't enjoy this with us," Annie said.

Alice nodded. "We should get something special to thank her for inviting us to go with Kate."

While Alice and Annie continued to scout out the lobby, Kate was motioned to the counter to sign the registration forms. After a long day on the road, she felt rumpled and plain standing in front of the sophisticated attendant in her sharp business suit, upswept hair, and perfect makeup.

"You're all set." The attendant, who identified herself as Adrian, handed Kate a copy of the registration form, a list of businesses located in the convention center, and room key cards. "Welcome to New York City."

Kate turned away from the counter and handed Annie and Alice a room key card. "Our room is on the forty-sixth floor," she said. The women moved to the elevator, which sped them to the top of the building. "Wow!" Kate exclaimed. "This is the tallest building I've ever stepped foot in."

The bellboy led the three friends to their room. Upon arriving there, he opened the door, stood back, and motioned to them to enter first. They went straight to the window and looked down on Times Square as he deposited their bags on luggage racks. After asking if he could be of any other assistance, he quietly accepted a tip from Annie and ducked out of the room.

"I can't believe we're here," Kate murmured, watching

people far below meandering around each other like ants raiding a picnic blanket. She kicked off her shoes, pulled her hair from its ponytail, and wrapped the band around her wrist before stretching out on the bed closest to the window. "I just need to doze a minute after that drive into the city."

*   *   *   *

Rested, refreshed, and dressed for urban adventure, Annie, Alice, and Kate slid into chairs around a high-top table in the hotel's casual but trendy restaurant, Frank's Place.

"I have a surprise for you," Annie said as soon as a handsome young server finished taking their food and drink orders. She pulled a paper out of her purse and set it in the middle of the table, grinning—thought Kate—like the Cheshire cat in Lewis Carroll's *Alice in Wonderland*. "The Avant-Garde is still going strong in Greenwich Village. According to these directions, we are but a mere thirty minutes or so away from a clue to the mystery singer's identity!"

Alice's jaw dropped while Kate reached for the paper, mentally preparing for returning to the streets of New York City in her van. Was she ready for it again so soon? Relief spread throughout her body when she saw the directions consisted of a twenty-minute train ride and a ten-minute walk. "No driving; that works for me! I'm up for an excursion to the club. You?"

Alice rubbed the back of her chair where her leather jacket was hanging. "Now I understand why you were so insistent about carrying our jackets to dinner. Just how long have you had this information about The Avant-Garde, anyway?"

The Cheshire cat grinned again. "Well, Ian mentioned Sunday that he had visited the club when he lived in New York several years ago. When I called LeeAnn Tuesday to tell her about the trip, she suggested I check to see if I could find it online. I did, and it was. I wanted to surprise you."

Shaking her head, Alice scanned the information Annie had printed about the club. "You sly dog! You sure are good at keeping secrets. It says here the club is still owned by the son of the man who founded it back in the 1930s. Wow, he must be getting up there in age now. Suppose he'd remember a singer from the forties?"

"Maybe," said Annie, pointing at a section about midway down the page. "According to the website, all of the jazz greats from the past six or seven decades have performed at this club. The venue is as legendary as the musicians who have played there."

Excited about the prospect of learning more about the mystery singer, Kate, Annie, and Alice chattered while sharing a sampler platter of appetizers.

Though still tired from the drive, Kate was rejuvenated by the thought of meeting the club's owner and what he might tell them. "I'm so glad you two came to New York with me." She folded her napkin and put it next to her empty plate. "I never would've ventured into Greenwich Village on my own. This is turning into a whole different adventure for me!"

*   *   *   *

"It's rather skinny for a legend, isn't it?" Alice cocked her head and looked up at the dark green awning stretching over the sidewalk connecting the narrow building to Seventh Avenue. "The awning looks like it might be bigger than the club."

Annie gave Alice's shoulder a good-natured nudge. "Don't judge a legend by its cover. And it's not about the building, silly. It's about the music. And this place has heard the best."

Kate stood in front of the battle-scarred, dark wooden door and looked back at Annie and Alice. "The doors don't open for another thirty minutes. Do you think we can get in?" She slowly tried the door and jumped with surprise when it opened. She held it ajar for Annie and Alice.

A shiver of excitement ran down Annie's spine. "I love this place already," she said. Oh, the stories these walls could tell! Framed color shots of contemporary artists Winton Marsalis, Chris Botti, and Sylvia Brooks led to backlit black-and-white portraits of heavy hitters like Louis Armstrong and Lena Horne, creating a welcoming committee of music who's-who lining the hallway from the front door to a stairway obviously leading to the club downstairs.

Alice motioned Kate and Annie to a group of portraits farther down the hallway. "Look at these. Don't they have a look similar to the photos Ernst Michaels printed for you? See the backlighting and curling smoke? They all have a moody look to them."

Studying the photos, Annie nodded. "I can't wait to see what we find downstairs."

They found a tall, wiry, middle-aged, ebony-skinned man with a bobbing Adam's apple, setting up the ticket booth. Introducing herself, Annie pulled out the matchbook and photos and explained the purpose for their visit.

He shuffled through the photos, smiled in recognition of the images, and pointed to an elderly man sitting alone near the stage. "You'll need to talk to the owner, Mitchell Grants. His family has owned the place for over seventy years. He grew up with these musicians. Let me see if he can speak with you."

The ticket booth attendant returned shortly. "Mr. Grants said he will see you now. His mind is like a steel trap, although his hearing is going. You'll have to speak up and talk clearly."

"Thank you so much." A jolt of excitement shot through Annie as she took the photos and matchbook cover from the man and surveyed the club. It was a dimly lit, tiny rectangle flanked on either side by a half dozen small square tables. The center was filled with round tables designed to seat four people. At the far end of the club, a line of lights illuminated a piano, drum set, and several microphones on the narrow stage. Framed record jackets lined the wood-paneled walls. Time stood still in this place. It looked just like the background of Leo Harmon's photos except for the noted absence of hazy cigarette smoke.

Mitchell Grants, a slight man dressed in a dapper suit, sat perusing a piece of paper under lamplight at a round table just left of the stage.

"Please sit." Grants motioned to three chairs. "What can I do for you? We have just a few minutes before the doors open."

After making introductions, Annie pulled the photos from her purse and recounted the story of finding the negatives. "A photojournalist in Maine, Ernst Michaels, said these looked

like the work of a jazz photographer named Leo Harmon.
There's one singer I don't recognize, and I found the negatives
of her photos mixed among my family portraits."

Grants, his bald head shining through thin gray hair,
sifted through the photos, stopping from time to time to
comment about a musician or explain the club's history. His
parents had opened the club in 1935, drawing musicians
from all over the country to perform different styles of jazz
music. Although he never played or sang music himself, he
grew up helping his parents run the place. As a young man,
he married a vocalist and eventually took over managing the
club. He inherited it when his parents died in the 1970s.

"That's my Gertrude, the fourth frame from the stage.
We ran the club together for years. Wasn't she beautiful?
She died several years ago, God rest her soul. But I just
couldn't bring myself to close or sell the place."

The raspy voice fell silent and Grants continued flip-
ping through the photos. Suddenly he stopped, blinked his
eyes in surprise, and said a single word, "Asta."

Annie leaned over to see which photo caused him to
react. "That's her, the mystery singer whose photo negatives
I discovered behind my grandparents' portrait! Who is she?"

Before he could respond, patrons began filling the club
and stopping by the table to pay their respects to Grants. He
looked up at Annie, Alice, and Kate, looking helpless as club
regulars commanded his attention. "I must attend to the
club now. Please stay and enjoy the music. If you come back
tomorrow night, I'll tell you the story of Asta. Come early."

The women agreed to return the next evening and
thanked Grants for inviting them to stay for the night's

performances. Shortly after he left the table, a young woman arrived with a round of soft drinks, compliments of the owner. Soon the friends were swept up into the sound of contemporary jazz music, a treat for Annie—a longtime jazz fan—and an education for Alice and Kate, whose tastes in music fell more toward classic rock and pop, respectively.

As soon as the bandleader announced a break, Kate threaded her way through the tables toward the restroom while Annie and Alice remained in their seats. "There is something magical about this place." Alice swirled the ice around her glass of cola. "I might even become a jazz connoisseur."

Annie laughed. "Now that would be some sort of magic!"

One by one, the musicians took their places on the stage, and a blushing Kate returned to the table. "We have another round of drinks coming. I met the nicest guy on my way back to the table. Actually, he is the trumpet player from the band. After we chatted a little, he said he'd buy us drinks if I promised to return tomorrow." She smiled shyly. "I didn't tell him we'd already decided to come back."

Alice looked at the stage as the drummer tapped out a beat, and the trumpeter casually lifted the horn to his lips. "He's cute too!"

A pink hue crept back into Kate's cheeks. "His name is Cole Cutchins. He's been performing here since he was a college student at Columbia University. He teaches music theory and jazz performance there."

Annie and Alice looked at each other and grinned. "Tomorrow will be an exciting night," Annie said.

～ 12 ～

Asta's dark eyes flashed as she stuck out her bottom lip and tossed long locks of hair behind her shoulders. "Don't be silly. There's no reason why I shouldn't continue singing. I love it, and the audience loves me." Her voice was calm and soft.

Her boyfriend, a few years her senior, placed a hand on her arm. The club's name blinked on and off in neon above them, casting an eerie glow on his face. "There's no need for you to do this. People like us don't parade ourselves onstage for the world to see." His words were icy but controlled. He gently pulled her into the shadows as Mitchell Grants hurried by and entered the club. "Being with me should be validation enough of your worth. You don't need the band or this club, and you certainly don't need men ogling you."

She took a deep breath and removed his hand from her arm. "This isn't about you or any other man. It's about me and how I feel when I sing. I have to go in and get ready for the show. Don't worry about the family name; people here just call me Asta." Falling silent a moment, she studied his face and tried to read it. "Will you stay for the show?"

He removed a cigarette from his pocket and lit it, throwing the spent match on the sidewalk between them. "I don't know. Maybe."

The smoke drifted between them, and Asta turned to leave. "I'll see you later."

The club was already buzzing with musicians warming up and patrons arriving for cocktails before the show. Creative electricity bounced between ice-filled glasses, cigarettes, and musical instruments. Asta walked through the club to a dressing room backstage and wondered how much Mitchell had overheard outside. Thirty minutes until showtime. Too late to find out.

The lone woman in the show, Asta had a dressing room to herself while the four band members shared a room across the hall. She enjoyed the quiet solitude before stepping onstage. It helped her tuck away one part of her soul and focus on the other. Her boyfriend's words echoed inside her. "I will not tolerate my family's good name being dragged down in association with a showgirl."

A showgirl? Is that how he saw her—as a fast and easy floozy, light on talent and heavy on makeup? All those years of classical voice and piano lessons, and he described her as a showgirl?

Applying a light dusting of powder, Asta studied her face in the mirror and squeezed her eyes shut to keep tears from falling. "A lady doesn't cry in public," she whispered. She blotted her lipstick and checked the bobby pins holding her blond curls to one side as the drumbeat filtered through the walls.

On cue, she stepped onto the stage, reveling in the spotlight, and poured her heart into the blues.

Mitchell and his father watched from the back of the club, smiling as the young singer commanded the attention of everyone in the room.

"This girl could be a star," the elder Grants said, nudging his son's arm.

"Uh-huh," Mitchell said, his eyes focused on the stage. "If she would ditch the rich boyfriend."

*   *   *   *

"They sure do feed us well here," Alice said, tossing paper cups and napkins into the trash can. "Fuel to keep us alert during the workshops. As if the ham-and-cheese croissant wasn't enough, the chocolate brownies were to die for."

Kate patted the waistband of her khaki pants. "We should have shared one sandwich among us. I ate too much."

Annie pulled her conference information packet from her bag and led the way to the exhibition hall. "We can walk it off in here before the afternoon session starts."

The huge hall was packed with fiber-art enthusiasts strolling among rows of booths, the hum of conversation almost drowning out the instrumental music piping through the sound system. Vendors from all over the country drew attention to their contributions to the fiber-arts realm with colorful displays, printed materials, creative dress, and varying degrees of persuasive conversation.

"Wow. This is overwhelming," said Kate, standing motionless in the doorway.

Alice chuckled as she linked her arm through Kate's and ushered her into the room. "This coming from the girl who drove us through New York City without flinching!"

Looking at the exhibition diagram in her packet, Annie devised a plan of attack. She pointed to a section of tables on one side of the room. "We have about three chances to see the exhibits. Let's go through these rows today. We can jump to the other side of the hall tomorrow and finish up the middle before we leave on Sunday. What do you think?" She looked at her watch. "We have about an hour before the next round of classes start."

Kate grabbed a small notepad and pen from her purse. "Mary Beth asked me to make a list of possible vendors for the shop."

The trio browsed through booths that tempted them with large varieties of hand-dyed yarn and fiber, knitting and crochet needles, quilt patterns, fiber dyes, and needle-felting supplies. They shared their experiences in the morning classes with one another until Annie disappeared into a display of machines that intertwined cutting-edge computer technology with various facets of the fiber-arts world. A few minutes later, a hands-on demonstration of how to create jewelry with fiber and beads lured Alice away long enough to start a necklace made from discarded fabric and an assortment of beads. Kate transformed into a butterfly, landing in one booth long enough to take a few notes before flitting to the next one. By the time Annie and Alice caught up to her, she had her notebook half-filled with suggestions for Mary Beth.

"You've been busy," said Annie, watching Kate flip through her pages of notes.

Alice pulled the necklace-in-progress from her bag. "I've been productive too, although making a necklace wasn't quite as exciting as Kate meeting that dreamy musician last night."

Annie and Alice exchanged a look and laughed as Kate

turned tomato red. "Oh stop it, you two. I'm not exactly a man magnet." She was smiling.

"Oh, no?" Alice said, widening her eyes. "You could have fooled me!"

Kate, unaccustomed to so much attention, looked down and shifted her weight from leg to leg. "Isn't it time for the next session of workshops to start? I'm ready to learn all about creative displays and marketing for the shop."

Annie consulted her packet and then her watch. "We have five minutes to get to our classes. When they are over, why don't we meet in our room to freshen up and call Mary Beth before we head to The Avant-Garde?"

*   *   *   *

"Oh, Mary Beth, you should see this place! Our room is beautiful." Kate stood at the hotel room window and gazed over Times Square, her cellphone held up to her right ear. "I wish you were here. How's the shop?"

Annie listened to Kate's end of the conversation as she exchanged her floral cotton blouse for a turquoise sweater in preparation for walking in the night air. She didn't feel the need to change her gray pants and sensible shoes.

"Annie, would you like to talk to Mary Beth?" Kate held out the phone.

Annie chatted with Mary Beth for a few minutes, describing the crocheting workshop she had attended and filling her in on the trip to the club. "I'm so sorry you couldn't attend the conference, but I'm thankful you sent Alice and me in your place. Speaking of Alice, do you have time to speak with her?"

Annie placed her hand over the phone. "Wow, you look fabulous! Here—say hi to Mary Beth."

Grabbing the phone, Alice mouthed "thank you" to Annie before addressing Mary Beth. "So I guess they already told you about Kate's flirtation last night." She paused and cast a guilty look toward the window. "Oh. Well, a good-looking musician sent us a round of drinks last night after she spoke to him during the band's break. Did they at least tell you that we found out the name of the mystery singer?" Alice sent a thumbs-up to Annie as she listened to Mary Beth. "We're going back tonight to see if we can make a connection between Asta, the Holdens, and Grey Gables. We'll let you know. OK. We'll call again. Bye!"

"You are so silly!" Annie grabbed a pillow from the nearest bed and hurled it at Alice. "I'm not so sure Kate wanted to tell anyone about the trumpet player."

Catching the pillow in time to prevent it from messing her hair and makeup, Alice punched it and tossed it back on the bed. "I'm really sorry, Kate. I figured one of you would have told her. Next to getting Asta's name, it was the highlight of the evening!"

Kate adjusted the red belt around her waist, the only concession to color in her white tunic and pants. Her dark hair fell in contrast against the tunic sleeves.

Alice stepped back and studied Kate's look. "You look beautiful, and I have the perfect pair of earrings to match your outfit!" She rummaged through her suitcase in search of her jewelry case. Minutes later, she held up a dainty pair of earrings, one earring in each hand, made of red, white, and black glass beads. Motioning Kate to the mirror over the dresser, Alice held an earring up to each of Kate's ears. "These will be stunning on you!"

Kate watched quietly as Alice slid the earring posts into her pierced ears then looked at her reflection in the mirror. "I usually don't wear dangle earrings. But they do look nice, don't they?"

"Alice was right," said Annie, peeking around Alice's shoulders to look into the mirror. "You look beautiful. You might attract the attention of a certain musician tonight!"

Putting an arm around each of her friends, Alice grinned. "My thought exactly!"

* * * *

"It's locked." Kate pushed on the door again and glanced back at Annie and Alice.

Alice reached over Kate's shoulder and rapped sharply on the door to The Avant-Garde. "They're expecting us. We just have to let them know we are here."

When the door finally opened, Cole Cutchins greeted them with a smile. "Welcome back! Come in; Mitchell is expecting you." He ushered the women in the door and locked it behind them. "We don't open for a while, so you have the whole place to yourselves."

Cole led them to the same table near the stage where they had sat the previous night. It was the owner's private table, he explained—had been for years. "This is where Mitchell holds court. No telling what musicians have sat in these chairs, everyone from John Coltrane to Chris Botti."

He pulled out a chair for each woman before grabbing a seat for himself. "What do you think of The Avant-Garde?"

The question was obviously addressed to Kate, so Annie ever so slightly nudged her friend's arm with an elbow. Kate looked into Cole's hazel eyes, leaned forward, and smiled. "There are a lot of ghosts here, I think. Not spirits, really, but sort of a musical echo from the past."

Annie watched Kate blossom and become animated in her own quiet manner, listening intently to Cole's stories, yet sporadically asking questions or making comments. They made an attractive couple, his blond head bent to her dark one as they exchanged ideas. How many romances began in this room with music magic?

"You came back—I'm so glad." Mitchell clasped each woman's hand before sitting in the empty chair between Alice and Cole. "I have a tray of drinks on the way."

"We wouldn't have missed this for the world." Alice moved her chair slightly to give him more room. "Asta's story has been elusive. We're anxious to hear it!"

Mitchell's eyes twinkled, and his large smile revealed two rows of almost too-perfect teeth. "Next to music, story-telling is my specialty. May I see the photos again?"

Annie handed him the stack. He quickly flipped through it until he found Asta's photo and stared at it a minute or two as if he were searching his mind for memories. "Asta was an enigma, cold and aloof around most people she met, but once she stepped onstage, she connected with the audience like nobody I've ever seen—and I've seen plenty."

The bartender placed a tray of drinks on the table. Mitchell waited until the ladies and Cole had taken a sip before he swirled his own glass and took a swig of whiskey. "Many men fell for Asta, but none as hard as Leo Harmon. Her voice could weave quite a spell."

Annie glanced at Alice, her heart racing at the sound of the photographer's name. "Did Leo Harmon meet Asta in the club?"

Nodding, Mitchell looked back down at the photograph and brushed his right index finger over the smoke hovering around Asta's head. "He was still dealing with the horror he experienced as a soldier during World War II when he walked in here the first time. Music and photography helped heal the wounds in his chest and his mind—and his heart, I suspect. He'd often show up to shoot photos in exchange for admission to the club. That's how we ended up with one of the largest collections of Leo Harmon photos in the world."

Alice bent her head to get a closer look at Asta's photo. "Did Asta and Leo get married?"

Mitchell fell silent and seemed lost in the past. He snapped out of it when Cole tapped his arm. "Asta and Leo? No, Asta was engaged to a wealthy young man who didn't appreciate jazz music or her singing in a nightclub. She never responded to Leo's affections, but she did revel in the attention he gave her. Asta never gave him a chance, but she inspired his artistry. I never saw any of Leo's photos that were more intense than those of Asta."

As Kate and Cole gazed at each other, Annie wondered how many musicians had fallen in love within these walls during the club's long history. "What happened to Leo and Asta?" she asked, impatient to hear the rest of the story.

Mitchell's eyes looked tired and sad. "When the Korean War broke out, Leo took a job as a war correspondent and was sent to Asia. He never returned. Asta sang here until she finished college and then left to marry her fiancé. As far as I know, she never sang again, but she had one of the most hauntingly beautiful voices I've ever heard."

Tears lurked in the corners of Kate's eyes. "That's so sad. Leo lost his love and his life, and Asta gave up her passion for a man and his money."

Members of Cole's band hovered near the stage and waved to get the trumpeter's attention. He looked at Kate. "More than a few loves have been found here. Some last and others don't. But all of them influence the music. Gotta go now. Will you stay and listen to our set?"

She hesitated and waited for nods from Annie and Alice. "Yes, we'd love to hear you play again. Thank you."

Mitchell watched Cole step onstage. "He's very talented, you know. We've been lucky; for seventy years, gifted musicians have found their way here."

"Legends attract talent. From what I understand, The Avant-Garde is a legend. What I don't understand," Annie said, gathering up her photos, "is how the negatives of Asta's photos ended up in my grandparents' portrait."

"That I can't explain," Mitchell said, pushing his chair out from the table. I need to tend to the club. It's been a pleasure visiting with you. Thanks for taking me down memory lane. Feel free to sit here and listen to Cole's group. They're very good."

The band opened with an instrumental number before Cole welcomed the audience to the club and introduced the next song. Placing his trumpet on its stand, he picked up a microphone and held it in the direction of his new friends. "This song goes out to Kate, and to Asta, wherever she is, for bringing Kate to The Avant-Garde."

Kate smiled and lifted her hand acknowledging Cole's gesture as he began to sing a love song. Her eyes didn't leave his face until he replaced the microphone in its stand.

Placing a hand on Kate's shoulder, Annie whispered in her ear. "Can you breathe?"

"Barely." It was the first time Annie had ever seen Kate that breathless. The second time came during the band's intermission.

"So what do you think?" Cole asked as he returned to his seat at the table.

Annie and Alice waited for Kate to answer. She blushed. "Nobody has ever dedicated a song to me before. It was beautiful. Thank you."

Cole beamed. "I wrote it myself. This was the first time it's been performed in public."

Alice grabbed her purse from the back of the chair. "Annie, let's go look at photos ... or something."

"Excuse us," Annie said, rising and draping her bag on one shoulder. "We'll be back in a few minutes."

After two paces she stopped, turned to Alice, and grinned. "That was smooth. Shall we look at portraits, or do you have some other mischief in mind?"

They walked to the other side of the room and paused in front of a portrait of a young Frank Sinatra. Alice angled her body to gain a clear view of Kate and Cole and left Annie facing Frank. "You are welcome to wander around the club if you like, but I'm going to stand right here and spy on them. And remember: We don't really know Cole Cutchins."

~ 13 ~

Water fell two stories in a shimmery sheet into the reflecting pool, sending rogue droplets into the air to land on people watching below. Waiting for Alice and Kate at their prearranged meeting spot, Annie sat on the bench and looked up in awe of the wall of water sliding down gold granite.

This was a different world.

The hotel's atrium was a paradox—the blend of light and tranquility from glass walls and the waterfall contrasted with the quick steps of people rushing from one place to another. Annie watched briefcase-carrying executives in business suits enter the upscale lounge and travelers browsing through attraction brochures. Groups of the convention attendees, arms laden with goodies from workshops, stopped at the hotel directory in search of the Grand Ballroom, where the fiber-arts fashion show was scheduled to begin in thirty minutes.

There was freedom in sitting still, an unknown amid the bustle, and watching the press of humanity. In Stony Point, where all eyes noticed your every move, this type of observation was nearly nonexistent.

Annie jumped when her cellphone began vibrating in the craft bag leaning against her thigh. She dug through workshop information sheets and yarn samples and snagged it before it stopped shaking. "Hello?"

"Annie?" Her heart lurched when she heard Ian's voice.

"Ian! How are things in Stony Point?" Annie put her hand over her free ear to block out the lobby noise so she could hear him better.

"Stony Point is quiet, especially compared to The Big Apple. I just left A Stitch in Time. Mary Beth said she talked to you yesterday. How's the conference?"

Annie waited for a large group of chattering women to pass before she answered. "Very informative. This morning I attended a workshop on needlecraft-related fundraisers and another on teaching methods for needlecraft classes. We have a lot to share with Mary Beth when we return home."

Ian cleared his throat. "Always thinking of the community. I like that. By the way, Mary Beth said you had been to the jazz club. Did you find out anything about the mystery singer?"

Annie had just finished telling Ian the story of Asta and Leo when Alice and Kate joined her by the waterfall. "Alice and Kate just walked up, so I need to get going. Thanks for calling to check up on us."

Waving to her friends, Annie mouthed Ian's name and pointed to the phone before ending the conversation. "I miss you too. See you soon! Bye."

Annie saw the mischievous look in Alice's eyes and opted to speak first. "Ian said everything is fine in Stony Point. He had just visited A Stitch in Time and talked to Mary Beth. He called to get an update on the mystery. He told me to say hi to y'all."

Kate sat on the bench next to Annie. "He's such a nice man. I never really gave much thought to elected officials, but he really does seem to care about the people of Stony Point, even when we aren't there." She pulled her cellphone from her purse. "I wonder if Vanessa called this morning." She flipped open the phone and paused before punching in her voice mail password. "Oh, it looks like I have a message from Cole." She listened to the message and grinned. "He asked for my cell number last night. He said he is looking forward to seeing me tonight and suggested we arrive in time to have dinner with him before the show. Isn't that sweet?"

Alice whipped out her own phone and accessed the Internet. Typing in "Cole Cutchins" and "trumpet," she discovered a number of entries. "Let's see if he's as real as he seems," she said. "Well, he *is* a professor at Columbia, and his band seems to be pretty popular in New York." She scrolled through several entries. "His students give him high ratings and describe him as cool, laid-back as a teacher but intense as a musician. No mention of a wife or fiancée. Looks good so far!"

Annie opened her mouth to mention the number of travel hours between New York City and Stony Point, but decided it was a bit premature. She opted to remind them of the fashion show instead. "Maybe we should head to the Grand Ballroom. We don't want to miss the opening run of the fashion show."

They chatted with other needlecraft enthusiasts on the way to the tenth floor. The conversation stopped when they stepped off the elevator into a fashion wonderland. The perimeter of the ballroom was lined with ficus trees and topiaries aglow with twinkling lights. An elevated runway cut a swath through rows of chairs and branched into a T at the front of the room. Greeters handed out programs as they entered the door.

"I am expecting Tyra Banks to appear at any moment," Alice quipped, her eyes roving the room. "I suppose we'd best find a seat. The room is filling up."

A plump, freckle-faced woman waved her program and motioned Annie to three chairs next to her near the center aisle just off the runway. "Look, there's Pam from Galveston, Texas! I met her in my crafty fundraiser class this morning. I think she's saved us seats."

Annie led the way to her new acquaintance. "Hi, Pam! These are the friends I told you about, Alice and Kate from Stony Point, Maine."

Pam held out her hand. "Hi, y'all. I sure am glad you arrived when you did. It was getting harder to keep people from taking these seats."

Alice took Pam's hand in her own. "Thanks for saving them. What a great view we'll have!"

Pam didn't miss a beat. "Anything for friends and family of Betsy Holden, God bless her. Years ago, I read an article about her in a needlework magazine. I wrote her a letter explaining how her work inspired me to open my own needle-craft store. She surprised me by writing the nicest letter in return. I hope I don't sound like some kind of groupie, but I have it framed in my shop."

Before Annie could respond, music started and the em-cee stepped to the microphone and welcomed the crowd before introducing the needlework experts who had created fashions for the show.

Annie tried to remain focused on the garments and

accessories flashing before her, but her mind kept floating back to Asta and Leo. What was their connection to Grey Gables? Grandpa spent time in New York after his Navy days, but that was before he met Gram. She thought of the photos of Grandpa she had found in the book about New York. What were the initials on them? She couldn't remember.

Suddenly, all the models poured onto the runway and the music became louder. Annie was startled from her reverie. It was time for the grand finale.

When the music ceased, Annie, Alice, and Kate thanked Pam again for saving their seats and told her they hoped to see her again before the end of the conference. During the elevator ride to the forty-sixth floor, Alice nudged Kate. "You're awfully quiet. Did you enjoy the fashion show?"

Kate answered after the elevator stopped to let three people off. "I must admit, I had a tough time concentrating. I couldn't stop thinking about Cole and the song he sang for me last night ... and the voice mail he left this morning. Is it possible to have feelings for someone you've just met?"

The question hung in the air before Alice finally answered it. "I don't know. Maybe. But I think it's worth a trip back to the club—don't you think so, Annie?"

Annie wasn't so sure she was the one to be giving relationship advice at the moment, and she wanted to change the subject. "I don't know. But I was lost in my own thoughts during the show. I just can't make the connection between Grey Gables and a jazz singer in New York City. It makes no sense."

They stepped off the elevator and walked to their room in silence, each woman lost in her own thoughts. When they entered the room, Alice went to her suitcase and retrieved three granola bars, while Kate sat on the couch and looked out over Times Square. Noticing the message light blinking on the hotel phone, Annie went to check the voice mail.

She punched the play button and listened to the sound of a man coughing before whispering, "This is Cole Cutchins. Tonight is not good for me after all. In fact, it's not a good time for you to be at the club."

"How odd! Listen to this." Annie pushed the replay button and turned on the speakerphone. The raspy voice filled the air. She played the recording twice before talking. "What do you think?"

Kate looked at her cellphone. "That doesn't sound like Cole. His voice is smooth as velvet. What time was that message left?"

Annie replayed the message and listened for the time. "Eleven o'clock this morning. What time did Cole call your cellphone?"

"One o'clock," said Kate, after double-checking the time. "Two hours after the message was left in the room. Suppose there's been a mistake? Should I call his cellphone?" She tugged nervously on a lock of hair resting on her shoulder. "What if he has changed his mind and doesn't want to see me again after all?"

Sitting down next to Kate, Annie pondered both messages in her mind. "He sounded pretty sincere in the message on your cellphone. And don't forget the song he dedicated to you last night."

Joining them on the couch, Alice handed each a granola bar. "Annie is right. Let's not jump to conclusions. I think we should stick to our plan and go to The Avant-Garde. I'll be surprised if he isn't thrilled to see you."

Thirty minutes later, they were dressed for the club and walking down Broadway to catch the subway.

"It really takes some planning to get anywhere in this city, doesn't it?" Kate said as they approached the stairs leading to the subway. "It's a whole different lifestyle. It's sort of exciting now, but I wonder if it would get old after a while."

Always up for adventure, Alice led the way to the turnstile. "I'm enjoying every second of this experience. It's not going to get old anytime soon!"

The subway car was not packed, but there were plenty of people in it, offering Annie some prime people-watching time. A handsome man with neatly trimmed black hair and large eyes sat near Alice and struck up a conversation. Alice was even more animated than usual. *Is she flirting with this man?* Annie wondered. By the time the twenty-minute ride was over, he knew that the women were visiting from Maine and this was their first trip to the city.

When the subway doors opened at their stop, Annie was surprised when the man rose to get off too. As they squeezed through the opening, he grabbed Annie's arm and held her back as Kate stepped off the train. Putting his mouth to her ear, he growled, "Keep that woman away from Cutchins if you know what's good for you!"

He was gone in a flash, leaving a trembling Annie to collect her wits.

Alice and Kate had stopped and waited for Annie to catch up with them before heading out of the subway station. "Annie? Are you OK? You look like you've seen a ghost," Alice said.

Annie double-checked to make sure her purse was still closed and her valuables safe. "Yes, I'm fine. But your Prince Charming just warned me to keep Kate away from The Avant-Garde and Cole. He shoved me pretty hard before he took off. I was so stunned I didn't see which way he went."

Blood drained from Kate's face. "First the phone message and now a warning to stay away from Cole? What's happening?"

"I don't know," Annie said, rubbing her arm where the assailant grabbed it. "I don't think he tried to take anything, but I am glad the negatives and matchbook cover are locked in Ian's office safe."

Kate was on the verge of tears. "Maybe we should catch the next train back to the hotel and just stay in tonight. We'll be safe there. Some things are just not meant to be."

Kate had had a turbulent marriage to Vanessa's father, but the unassuming woman had come out of her shell when she was around the warm and friendly musician. Annie was determined to get her back to the club to see him. "I'm fine. Really, I am. And you will be too. The club is a short walk from here." Fear was not going to rule her!

Everything seemed normal now. Nobody seemed to notice the three shaken women. Annie tried to shrug off her sense of foreboding. Who was trying to keep them away from the club? And why?

— 14 —

Kate stood in the back of the dark club, immobilized by the sight of Cole standing alone on the stage, his trumpet pointed upward and gleaming in the yellow spotlight. Her fear dissipated—the incident on the subway forgotten—as she listened to note after note float into the air.

"That's beautiful." She just wanted to watch him unnoticed and burn the memory in her mind forever.

She felt Alice lean against her shoulder. "Do you mean the man or the music?"

A smile tugged at Kate's lips. "Both. They are both beautiful."

"Can't argue with you there," Alice said with a soft laugh.

"Me either," Annie whispered in Kate's other ear.

They stayed in the shadows, wordlessly listening to the music, until Annie sneezed at the same time Cole took a breath after a long run of notes. He looked up and squinted into the darkness. "Hello?"

Kate stumbled as Alice pushed her forward with a whisper. "Go on, answer him."

"Hi, Cole. We got here a little early." Kate hesitated and searched for the right words to say. "We've been enjoying your music. Um, we didn't mean to spy on you."

He put his trumpet on its stand and stepped off the

stage. "Kate! I didn't see you come in. Welcome back, ladies. And I know you weren't spying."

The club was quiet, absent of clientele and musicians—except for Cole. The women had once again gained admission via the ticket taker who by now recognized them immediately. Though the room was dim, and Kate couldn't see the portraits, she felt the eyes of long-dead musicians peering from the walls. They lived on in the music played by a new generation of musicians. "Do you ever feel like they are watching you, the old jazz musicians?"

Cole turned his head toward the smiling Louis Armstrong. "They listen too. I play better in this room than I do anywhere else, even the recording studio at the university." He paused. "I'm glad you made it here early. I have time to take you to dinner at Marvin's, my favorite local café. It's right around the corner." He led them back upstairs to the club's entrance and pulled a key ring from his pocket. "Mitchell gave me a key to the place a long time ago," he explained. With that, the group stepped back out into the night, and Cole locked the front entrance to The Avant-Garde.

*   *   *   *

Fifteen minutes later, the four of them were sitting around a table, sharing a nook with an old pay phone from the days when it cost a dime to make a call. The walls were lined with old photos, vintage plates, and Greenwich Village memorabilia.

"This place is lovely," said Annie, studying several

miniature bronze busts sitting atop a small wooden shelf on the wall opposite the phone.

Alice, sitting next to Annie, was amazed to see a pay phone on the wall. "Wow, what a relic! I'm glad they kept it, though. There aren't many of those around anymore. This place sort of reminds me of Grey Gables with all of the old stuff here."

The women laughed, and Annie quickly gave Cole an abbreviated history of Grey Gables and the never-ending mysteries provided by the attic. "We are definitely history buffs."

Cole pointed out a series of photos displayed near the entrance of the café. "It's been owned by the same family since 1919. Each generation is represented on that wall. History lives here just like it does at The Avant-Garde."

Alice excused herself and left the table. By the time she returned, the server had left several plates of food.

"Annie, I need you to see something. It won't take long. Your food won't get cold."

"Alice, this isn't a spy game, is it?" Annie asked with a smile while refolding her napkin and putting it by her plate. She looked at Cole and Kate. "If you'll excuse me, I'll indulge Alice a minute. Please go ahead and start eating."

Annie followed her friend as they threaded their way through the tables toward the back of the café. "The restroom is rather small, and I had to wait my turn, which gave me time to find this." Alice led Annie through a set of tied-back burgundy curtains into a small hallway lined with framed snapshots of days gone by. She pulled a section of the curtain from the wall and there, between portraits of Charlton Heston and Grace Kelly, was a black-and-white photo of Asta between two young men, one tall and the other rather short. "Isn't this Asta? Who are these guys with her?"

Leaning closer to the photo, Annie breathed a sigh of relief. "Yes, it's Asta. But neither of them is Grandpa. I never really thought he had been interested in anyone but Gram. You know, this looks like the photos of Leo Harmon that I found online. But if it *is* Leo, I wonder who took the photo?" The man was too tall to be Grandpa, although his hair was also dark, and while his smile was pleasant, it just didn't have the Holden family look. The other man was too short, his grin too wide. "Maybe the shorter man is Mitchell. He has that toothy-smile thing going."

"Maybe. No telling." Alice stuck her head through the doorway and looked around. "The coast is clear. Let's take a picture of it!"

"You are incorrigible," Annie replied, holding back the curtain for her friend.

Alice chuckled. "Yes, and you love that about me." She snapped several photos of the print using her cellphone. "I suppose we should get back to the table," she said. "We don't want Kate and Cole to think we are on a spying expedition!"

Annie took one more peek at the photo before returning the curtain to its place. "Well, I suppose we can sneak back to the table and see if we catch those two making goo-goo eyes at each other."

"Mission accomplished," said Alice, brushing her hands together in an all-finished signal. "I'm glad you are getting into this matchmaker thing."

Annie raised her eyebrows. "Oh, is that what we're doing?"

Kate and Cole were engrossed in conversation when Annie and Alice returned to the table.

"We're back!" Alice announced as she plopped down in her chair. "I was right. There is a photographic treasure right here in this restaurant!"

Cole put down his fork. "There are lots of photos in this place, many of them taken at The Avant-Garde over the years. What did you find?"

Alice shifted in her chair as if about to explode with information, reminding Annie of Peggy when she was about to pop from keeping a secret. "I peeked behind the tieback curtains in the hallway—I always look behind curtains because you never know what you'll find. There was a photo of Asta and Leo. At least, Annie thinks it's Leo, based on pictures she found of him online. He was one tall, lanky dude. Handsome in a quirky sort of way."

Reaching for a slice of bread and dipping it into a small bowl of olive oil, Annie thought it was time to bring up the handsome ruffian on the subway. "Cole, do you have any idea why someone would not want you to get to know Kate?"

"Of course not," Cole said, his ravioli-laden fork stopped midway to his mouth, "but that's a strange question. Why?"

The women told him about the phone message left in the hotel room and described the incident on the subway.

"That's odd. I didn't leave a message on the hotel-room phone. I called Kate's cellphone," Cole said. "The man on the subway, did he try to hurt you?"

Annie shook her head and rubbed her hand over the spot where the ruffian grabbed it. "No, not really. I mean, he shoved me a little, and I probably have a nasty-looking bruise on my arm."

"Did you call 911?"

"No, we didn't, because nothing was stolen, and I wasn't badly hurt. It scared us though." Annie looked at Cole. "Are there any jealous exes lurking around?"

"I hate to admit this, but I've not had a serious girlfriend in ages. No worries in the jealous ex department." He glanced at Kate before addressing Annie. "Do you think all of this could have anything to do with the photos you unearthed?"

"Maybe," Annie said. "Anything is possible. But why would photos from over fifty years ago cause someone to go to these lengths to scare us away?"

Cole shrugged. "Beats me. I didn't know Asta existed until you showed up with Leo Harmon's photos of her. My only connection is Ernst Michaels. Mitchell told me you had some photos printed by him. Ernst and I met at Columbia years ago."

Alice whipped out her cellphone and signed onto the Internet. "I wonder whatever happened to Asta." Her fingers punched keys with rapid speed. The words *Asta* and *jazz singers* didn't turn up anything. Neither did *Asta* and *obituary*. "Strange. I don't remember Mitchell giving us her last name, do you?"

Kate pushed her plate away. "Now that you mention it—no, he didn't. Maybe she started the one-name thing long before Cher or Madonna. But how many jazz singers named Asta can there be? How do you suppose someone disappeared in the 1940s? Did she take her own life? Have children? Move to Paris?"

Growling with irritation, Alice stuffed the cellphone in her purse. "What good is technology when it doesn't give you the answers you need?"

After kicking around several possible reasons for the phone message and the incident on the subway and their possible connection to Asta, the conversation ceased. Four half-finished meals were left on the table. Cole signaled the server for the check and took his wallet from his pocket. "This is on me, a thank-you for coming to hear me play tonight. And I intend to escort you back to the hotel after the show. I want to make sure you're safe. I'm only playing in the first set, so it won't be too late."

*   *   *   *

Cole had just finished his set when Mitchell Grants stopped by the table to see Annie, Alice, and Kate. "You came back to see us. You've been bitten by the jazz bug." He kissed each of them on the cheek as they rose to greet him.

Alice snickered. "Jazz bug, love bug. Lots of bugs buzzing around this club these days."

Giving Alice a light swat on the arm, Kate interrupted before more could be said. "We've enjoyed meeting you, Mr. Grants. Thank you for everything."

Recorded music filtered through the speakers as the band members stepped from the stage. Mitchell looked around the club before turning to Annie. "Thank you for sharing your photos with me. You really took me down memory lane. Those were the glory days of jazz."

Removing the napkin from beneath her empty glass,

Annie neatly printed her name and phone number before handing it to Grants. "If you remember anything else about Asta or hear from her family, please give me a call."

He stuffed the napkin in the inside pocket of his sports coat, his gnarled fingers shaking a bit. "When Asta stepped down from that stage after her last show here, we never saw her in The Avant-Garde again. It was like she just vanished. But if I hear of anything, I'll let you know."

Club patrons were streaming in for the next set by the time Cole led Kate and her friends from the building. "I'm springing for a cab. It's safer."

"You won't get any complaints from us," Kate said with a sigh. "I was dreading getting back on that subway."

Cole pointed out places of interest on the way to the convention center and took Kate's hand in his about five minutes into the trip, which went much faster than the trek on the subway. She dreaded saying goodbye and wondered if she would ever see him again.

When the cab pulled under the portico at the convention center, Cole read the fare total, selected a twenty-percent tip, and swiped his credit card in the machine anchored in the backseat.

"Thank you for seeing us home, Cole, but you don't need to walk us to the room. We'll be fine." Annie was already digging her room key out of her purse.

He walked ahead to the door and held it open for them. "I'll just feel better if I actually hear that door lock behind you. Besides, I'm not quite ready to say goodbye yet."

Although it was after eleven o'clock, the hotel lobby was filled with people arriving to visit one of the several restaurants and clubs in the center. Kate couldn't imagine starting a night out so close to midnight, but she was glad Cole didn't want to say goodbye.

She squeezed his hand. "I'm glad you're here."

The elevator darted to the forty-sixth floor. When the doors opened, Cole held Kate's hand tightly and held her back a moment to allow Annie and Alice to walk ahead of them toward the room.

Annie slid her room key into the slot on the door and opened the door before looking back at Cole. "Thank you for dinner and the escort. We've had an exciting weekend."

Stepping one foot in the room, Alice looked back with a grin. "Don't stay out too late, kids! And thanks for everything, Cole."

When the door closed, Cole traced Kate's cheek and pressed a business card into her hand before lightly kissing her lips. "I'd like to see you again."

Heart pounding and a bit flustered, Kate opened her mouth to respond, but before the words would come out, the hotel room door flew open.

"I'm sorry to interrupt," Alice said, as Cole and Kate jumped apart, "but you both need to come inside. There's a problem!"

~ 15 ~

Annie, Alice, and Kate stood speechless, taking in the shocking scene inside the hotel room. Their suitcases had been thrown open and tossed aside, the contents strewn all over the room. Sheets had been torn from the bed, and mattresses were askew on the box springs. Contents of three cosmetic cases had been emptied onto the bathroom floor.

Cole put an arm around a trembling Kate while Annie picked up the phone to call the front desk. Yanking her trusty cellphone from her bag, an uncharacteristically quiet Alice began snapping photos, working from the door of the room toward the window and then backtracking to the bathroom.

Replacing the receiver on the phone, Annie turned around and slowly surveyed the disarray. "They said to not touch anything in the room. Hotel security will contact NYPD, and both will be here soon."

She watched Kate struggle to maintain composure and was impressed when Cole casually suggested the couple wait outside the room for the authorities to arrive. The door had just closed behind them when Alice growled from the bathroom.

"Really? Was it really necessary for them to break my brand-new bottle of perfume and empty a brand-new jar of makeup into the sink?" She continued snapping away, the camera's flash bouncing off the mirror. "Do you suppose the hotel will reimburse us for damages?"

A tap at the door interrupted Alice's tirade. Annie reached for the doorknob. "Maybe this is someone who can answer that question for you."

She opened the door to find a New York Police Department police officer presenting his badge and a uniformed hotel security guard holding a clipboard. Kate and Cole entered the room behind them. "I'm Annie Dawson. Thank you for coming so quickly."

Annie introduced Alice and Kate and explained their reason for being at the hotel. "We are a bit unnerved, as you can imagine," she said. "Oh, this is Cole Cutchins. He was nice enough to escort us back to our room after an evening at The Avant-Garde."

The police officer, a small man with piercing eyes and a thin nose, nodded and handed Annie a business card. "I'm Officer Frank Fox, NYPD, and this is Hal Bassett, the hotel security chief."

Alice tittered nervously and whispered, "Cool, we have the Fox and the Hound, a regular Disney movie!"

Neither Fox nor Bassett looked amused. While Bassett checked the closet and dressers, Fox walked to the far side of the room and jotted notes on a pad. "Someone really did a number on your room. Were any of you here when the intruders entered?"

The three women and Cutchins shook their heads.

Fox scribbled on his pad. "Who discovered the room had been ransacked?"

"Alice and I came in the room first. Kate and Cole were in the hallway," Annie said.

Each woman took turns describing the evening from the time they left The Avant-Garde to the minute Annie picked up the phone to call the hotel's security office.

When they finished, Fox walked through the room, taking care to step over the items scattered on the floor. "Can you tell if anything is missing?"

Kate, who had been quietly clinging to Cole during questioning and speaking only when directly addressed, finally found her voice. "That's what is so weird. It doesn't look like anything was taken. Annie's jewelry case was untouched, and I had a few gas-station gift cards tucked in my bag. None of them was missing."

"Any idea who would have done this?" Fox looked at each of the women before settling his eyes on Cole. "What about you?"

The musician squeezed Kate's hand. "I think you need to tell him everything that's happened today." He looked at Officer Fox. "Someone has been trying to keep us apart."

Kate described the two conflicting phone messages received earlier in the day, and Annie gave a blow-by-blow description of the subway incident.

While Bassett and Fox completed their reports, the crime-scene squad arrived to take fingerprints, and the hotel manager, Bradley Ford, stopped in to offer the women a different room and assure them they'd be safe for the duration of their stay. Bassett, he said, would have a security guard posted outside their room all night.

"I sincerely apologize for what happened here tonight,"

Ford said. "Our security is second to none, and I assure you this type of thing rarely happens. I'll have an incident report for you to sign before you check out in the morning." He referred to his notes before addressing Kate. "I understand you signed for the room representing the business A Stitch in Time. Is that correct?"

Kate nodded. "Yes. I can sign the report for you."

"I know it is late, but please write a list of damaged or stolen items and bring it with you when you visit the front office to sign the report." Ford's eyes moved back and forth between Kate, the person who signed the room agreement, and Annie, who had done most of the talking since he arrived. "We'll need both the list and report to submit with paperwork to the insurance company." He had all of the sincerity of a businessman protecting his paycheck.

Ford and Cole accompanied the women to their new room on the twenty-fourth floor.

"If you need anything at all, please call my cellphone, and I'll personally see to it." Ford handed Kate a business card with a cellphone number circled in red ink. "A security guard will be down shortly to escort you back to your old room to retrieve your things after the police department finishes up. He will then remain outside your room until morning."

After Kate closed the door behind the hotel manager, Cole put his arm on her shoulder. "Would you like me to stay here tonight? On the couch, of course."

"No thanks, Cole," said Kate. "We'll be OK."

Annie looked at the bedside clock and was surprised to see it was after 1 a.m. "It's getting late, and we're all exhausted, Cole," she said. "We appreciate the offer, but we will be fine, especially with a guard right outside our door."

Kate nodded. "I'll call you tomorrow and let you know everything is all right."

The couple slipped out of the room to say goodbye in private.

"If we can't get our stuff from the old room soon, I'm going to sleep in these clothes," Alice said, plopping on the couch and gazing out the window. "Look at the people milling around at nearly 2 a.m. Don't these people ever sleep? Oh, wait a minute—I guess that's why they call it the city that never sleeps."

Alice was just starting to doze off when a blushing Kate returned from the hallway. She perked up when the door banged shut. "Oh, you look mighty smiley for someone whose room was just ransacked."

Kate leaned back on the door a moment and closed her eyes before crossing the room and joining Alice on the couch. "Well," she said rubbing her eyes, "it isn't often you get a mysterious phone call, have your room burglarized, and get kissed by a gorgeous musician—all in the same day."

Getting her second wind, Alice raised her eyebrows. "Did you say kissed?"

Annie chuckled. "I believe that is exactly what she said."

"Well, he kissed me twice, actually," Kate said with a shy smile.

"Just when did you have time for all this kissing, anyway?" Alice was suddenly wide awake and wanting details.

A sharp knock echoed through the room. Alice opened the door and Chief Bassett stepped into the room. "We're finished upstairs," he said. "I'll take you back to collect your belongings now."

*   *   *   *

Despite a nearly sleepless night, Annie woke in time to shower and dry her hair before her cellphone sounded the eight o'clock alarm she had set for each morning of the conference. Kate wasn't far behind her, and even Alice was up as soon as the alarm went off.

While waiting for her friends to get ready, Annie sat on the bed and called Mary Beth to give her a rundown of the night's events. Shortly after she hung up the phone, a yawning Alice emerged from the bathroom.

"Are you sure your alarm didn't go off early? It sure feels like we just went to sleep," Alice grumbled.

Kate passed by on her way from the bed to the shower. "At least you two managed to sleep a few hours. Every time I closed my eyes, I pictured strangers throwing stuff out of our suitcases. I doubt I slept an hour all night."

Annie looked at her friends with sympathy. "I think I was so exhausted that even a nightmare couldn't have wakened me."

Before they could respond, Annie's cellphone rang. She reached back to the nightstand where she had left the phone after talking to Mary Beth. "It's Ian," she said, her words mixed with joy and surprise.

"Hello, Ian. I'm so glad you called."

"Mary Beth just called to tell me about what happened. She's worried about you and so am I. Are you all right?" Ian asked, his voice calm but laced with concern.

"Yes, we are all fine. A bit shaken, but fine. But thank you for calling and checking on us. I promise I'll let you know when we are home."

"Annie, please be very careful and stay safe. You are very important to me."

Annie hesitated and turned her back to the room. "You're important to me too. Goodbye, Ian."

Dressed in jeans and casual long-sleeved shirts for comfortable travel, they left their packed bags in the room and grabbed breakfast in the buffet line set up for conference attendees near the exhibition hall. After greeting other crafters they had met during the weekend, the trio took their breakfast to a corner table and ate while completing the list of damaged items Chief Bassett requested.

Kate passed the list first to Alice and then to Annie to make sure she had included everything.

Alice scanned the list as she shook her right arm, sending several bangle bracelets clanking from her wrist toward her elbow. "Makeup, perfume, and lotion bottles. Everything is here except my jewelry case. They broke the zipper when they tore it open. Isn't it weird that nothing was stolen? What do you suppose they were searching for?"

After reading the list and returning it to Kate, Annie spread some butter on what was left of her biscuit. "Beats me. The main thing is the damage to my suitcase; the zipper and lock were broken." With the morsel halfway to her mouth, she dropped it on her plate. "When Ian and I went to pick up the photos from the photojournalist in Petersgrove, he told us to keep the negatives in a safe place because they are considered valuable in certain circles.

That could be a connection. At any rate, I am glad they are tightly locked in Ian's safe."

"Well, I don't know if there is a connection or not, but those photos led us to The Avant-Garde and Cole, so they are invaluable to me!" Kate looked at her watch and grimaced. "As much as I'd love to stay in New York, we really need to get going. I want to get home to Vanessa as soon as possible. Maybe I should give her a call and tell her what happened before she hears it from someone else."

Walking to the front desk, Annie asked for Mr. Ford while Alice caught the eye of a bellboy.

"I'll grab all our bags and meet you here after you two finish the paperwork with Mr. Ford," Alice said, digging her room card out of her purse. "I'll be back in a jiff."

Fifteen minutes later, the women were standing under the portico, waiting for the valet parking attendant to retrieve Kate's van. Annie looked back at the imposing building and recalled the moment they first arrived—was it just three days ago?

"Wow, a lot has happened since we dropped off the van on Thursday," she said. "But we didn't get much sightseeing done."

Alice crossed her arms, stuck out one leg, and tapped her toe on the sidewalk. "Do you mean to tell me this trip wasn't exciting enough for you? You want to play tourist too?"

Their laughter filtered through the morning breeze.

"But what's a near-mugging on the subway or a ransacked hotel room compared to the thrill of climbing the Empire State Building or walking the Brooklyn Bridge?" Annie asked, remembering the photos of

Grandpa tucked inside the book in the Grey Gables library. "History is exciting."

"All of your mysteries have turned you into a thrill seeker, Annie," Alice said, her eyes twinkling. "Next thing you know, you'll want to head to the big city in search of more dangerous challenges! A mystery at the Statue of Liberty perhaps?"

The women grabbed their crafting totes from the bag cart as the attendant pulled Kate's van up to the portico.

"Annie doesn't need dangerous challenges to make a trip back to New York. Now we can return to see Cole," said Kate, sliding open the back door and tossing her tote into the seat. "We'll have our own personal tour guide."

Annie and Alice exchanged a look and laughed. "Yeah, right," they said in unison.

Watching the bellboy load the bags into the back of the van, Alice offered to drive the first shift home. "Why don't you catch up on your sleep and take the wheel in a couple of hours?"

Kate stretched and looked longingly at the backseat. "That sounds good, actually. Even as tired as I was last night, I still tossed and turned." She handed the valet her claim ticket, climbed into the roomy backseat, and took off her jacket before buckling her seatbelt.

Annie pulled several bills from her wallet and divided them between the bellboy and the valet, who opened the passenger door before taking the tip from her hand.

Kate looked back at the hotel as Alice maneuvered the van onto the street. "By the way, Mr. Ford apologized for our trouble and gave me a gift card for two free nights in the hotel, so Annie, we will come back sometime to see your historical landmarks."

"Home again, home again, jiggety-jig," Annie recited as Kate, who had taken the wheel somewhere just past the Massachusetts-New Hampshire line, turned the van into the driveway leading to Grey Gables.

"To market, to market, to buy a fat hog, home again, home again, jiggety-jog," finished Alice, leaning forward with her elbows on the back of Annie's seat. "Do you suppose Betsy knows how much we quote her nursery-rhyme quips from our childhood?"

Annie looked at Grey Gables and sighed with relief at being home after such a whirlwind trip. "I prefer to think so. I see her as my personal guardian angel." She collected her place mat in progress, along with a ball of yarn and a hook, and put them in her tote bag as Kate pulled up to the walkway to the house. "Kate, you drove like a pro in New York, just like you'd been in the concrete jungle your entire life."

"And she did pretty well in the flirting department too," said Alice, sliding open the passenger door.

Giggling, Kate switched off the ignition. "I did, didn't I?" She unbuckled her seatbelt and opened the van door. "Do you mind if I use your restroom before I head home?"

"Sure you may. Y'all come in and freshen up before you take off. Boots will love the extra company after being cooped up alone for several days." Annie pulled her suitcase from the back of the van and then stepped out of the way so Alice could retrieve hers.

Walking up the path to the house, Alice asked what they should share with the Hook and Needle Club ladies first—Kate's romance, an update on the Asta mystery, or information gathered at the convention. "I vote for the romance," Alice said, "but Asta runs a close second. Everyone will want to know what we found out about her."

"Well, we did go to New York to represent Mary Beth at the convention. Perhaps we should start with that," Kate insisted.

Annie stopped in her tracks and held her rolling bag upright. "Or we could start with explaining why my front door is wide open."

They stood on the walkway and looked at each other.

"What do we do?" Kate looked at Annie.

Alice whipped out her phone and called 911 as Annie started toward the porch. "Umm, Annie. They said to stay outside."

Annie stopped on the front step and studied the house. She was grateful to Breck for turning on the front porch light. "Nothing looks broken. The windows are fine. The doorknob looks OK."

"Yes, but we don't know what or who we will find inside, especially after the episode at the hotel. I'll feel much better if we all go back and wait in the van," Alice said, waving her phone and taking backward steps toward the driveway. "Chief Edwards will be here in a minute."

The police chief showed up not too long after they locked themselves in the vehicle. "Is everyone OK?" he said as Kate rolled down her window. "I know it's getting dark, but have you seen any movement around the house?"

"No," the women said in unison.

Chief Edwards asked a few more questions and jotted down some notes before telling the women to stay in the van while he searched the house. When his backup, Officer Cal Peters, arrived, the two men disappeared in the darkness.

After what seemed an eternity to Annie, Chief Edwards returned while the young officer searched the yard. "The house isn't ransacked. On the surface, anyway, everything seems to be as you left it. But I'd like you to come in and walk through it with me just to make sure nothing is missing."

Walking through the house, Annie felt a curious sense of déjà vu, and not just from the hotel break-in. How many times had the chief been called to Grey Gables since she had started unearthing mysteries in the attic? But the jazz singer mystery didn't appear to involve valuable stocks, jewelry, art, or missing people like the others had.

"How odd. There's nothing missing," Annie said, stepping into the kitchen and finding the cat's filled food and water bowls. "Except Boots! Has anyone seen Boots?"

Annie sank down in a chair, propped both elbows on the kitchen table, and put her head in her hands. This was too much—The Kiss, the man on the subway, two break-ins, and now a missing Boots. Tears welled in her eyes, and she wiped them away with her index fingers. Taking a deep breath, she said a silent prayer. *Dear God, thank You for keeping us safe during our trip to New York. Please watch over Boots—keep her safe and bring her home to me.*

"Annie, we're going to look for Boots. But Kate just

mentioned that someone had broken in and ransacked your hotel room in New York, and Alice told me about the subway incident." Chief Edwards placed a hand on her shoulder. "I need to ask you a few questions while Officer Peters looks for the cat."

Annie had just finished telling the chief what she remembered from the New York incidents when Kate entered the kitchen, cellphone in hand. "I need to get home to Vanessa. Are you going to be all right?"

"Of course she'll be all right, because I will be here with her all night," said Alice as she walked through the doorway from the hall. "After all, my suitcase is already here."

Annie hugged Kate. "Go home to Vanessa and give her a hug for me. Don't worry. I'll be fine."

Officer Peters returned to the house carrying Alice's suitcase, having found it outside the van while searching the house. He hadn't seen any signs of Boots. After assuring Annie he would drive by the house at regular intervals throughout the night, Officer Peters left to resume his patrol duty. Chief Edwards told Annie he would request a copy of the police report from NYPD the next morning to see if there was a connection between the two incidents. After he said goodnight, Annie and Alice stood at the window and watched his flashlight bob in the darkness as he took one more look around the front yard.

*   *   *   *

Annie woke slowly, surprised to see the sun filtering through the curtains. Half asleep, she stretched and

patted the sheets, feeling for Boots. Her eyes flew open
when she remembered arriving home the previous night
to find Boots missing. Jumping from the warm blankets,
Annie ran to the window, hoping to see a glimpse of the cat
in the yard. Nothing moved in the yard except trees and
plants waving in the wind. She threw on a pair of jeans
and a sweatshirt and ran downstairs. Grabbing her jacket
and sliding into her yard boots, she went out the mudroom
door, calling for Boots.

When she started losing her voice, Annie returned with
a heavy heart to the kitchen to find a full coffeepot and
Alice removing a batch of apple muffins from the oven.

"You, my friend, are one of the very few people I'd wake
up for at such a beastly time after two consecutive nights
of very little sleep," Alice teased, shaking a crocheted pot
holder at her. Then her face softened. "How are you doing?"

Annie retrieved two mugs from the cabinet and filled
them with coffee. She handed one to Alice. "I'm worried,
tired, and a little sad. I wonder where Boots is."

"I'll help you look some more after we have a bit of sustenance. And I guess I should put some clothes on before I
go tromping around the neighborhood." Alice dumped the
muffins into a basket lined with a tea towel and set them on
the table. "Sit."

Annie sat.

Alice grabbed two plates from the counter and joined
her at the table. "Now, how are you? Really."

"To be honest, while I am a bit unnerved about the two
break-ins, right now I am more concerned about Boots. We
have no way of knowing how long or why she's been gone."

Annie nibbled a muffin but mostly picked at the topping. "I just hope she's safe."

"You haven't said much about Ian through all of the excitement. Are you dealing with that any better?"

"Well, I'm still struggling some," Annie admitted, pushing a crumb around her plate with her left index finger. "But I know Wayne would want me to be happy. I have to admit that, as stressed out as I was Saturday night in the hotel room, I nearly melted when I heard Ian's voice the next morning."

"That's a start. It's been fun watching your friendship with Ian grow. Didn't you get a kick out of seeing Kate flirt with Cole?"

"Yes, he did draw her out of her shell." Annie stopped playing with the crumbs and put a bite in her mouth. She looked at the bowl of cat food waiting near the door. "I hope I see Boots again. I'm really worried."

Alice covered the muffin basket with a towel before taking the cups to the sink. "Now that we've had our coffee, how about we go look for her before heading into town?"

~ 17 ~

*T*he "Closed" sign was up at A Stitch in Time, and Annie hesitated before trying the door. "Do you suppose she's ready for visitors even if she's not open for business?"

Alice peered through the glass, shading her face with one hand and clutching a paper bag with the other. "I think we are more like family, and she'd like to see us whether or not we can buy anything."

She had just backed away from the door when it flew open with Mary Beth on the other side. "Am I glad to see you!" she said, hugging Alice and then Annie. "I've been so worried. Kate's here. She filled me in on everything. Has Boots returned?"

Fighting the tears threatening to fill her eyes, Annie shook her head. "Alice and I searched inside and out of Grey Gables for over an hour this morning. No sign of her."

Kate materialized from the back of the shop. "How are you? Any sign of Boots?"

"No," Annie and Alice said in unison.

Annie surveyed the damage in the shop. It looked worse than it had before the convention. Water stains created a roadmap down the back wall leading to the discolored wood floor. The front of the shop along the window and behind the checkout counter was filled with neat pyramids of boxes, and a few plastic containers encroached into the main area of the store. Obviously, merchandise had been boxed and moved as more leaks had emerged. "When will you be able to open for business?"

A drill pierced the relative quiet with a high-pitched metallic sound, reminding Annie of trips to the dentist.

Mary Beth waited for the noise to stop before she answered. "They're working on the roof today. I hope Wally will be here tomorrow to look at the floor and walls."

Peggy's husband, Wally, was well known around town for his innate talent for renovation. He had done or supervised most of the work on Grey Gables. Annie knew the shop was in good hands.

Alice walked to the checkout counter and placed the paper bag on it just beneath a spot on the wall where a collection of thimbles was mounted. Mary Beth had inherited the thimbles from her grandmother, had put them in the shadow box, and had kept collecting them in her honor.

"I think we have something that might cheer you up a bit," Annie said.

Alice reached into the bag and pulled out a small wrapped package about the size of a ring box and handed it to Mary Beth. "A token of our love and affection," Alice said, handing the box to the shopkeeper with great ceremony.

Mary Beth looked at the package sitting in the palm of her hand. "Did you take a trip to Tiffany's?"

"Don't be silly," said Alice, the jewelry aficionado. "One simply does not gift-wrap a blue Tiffany's box!"

Laughing, Mary Beth untied the small bow and removed the tape from the bright floral wrapping paper. She laughed even harder when she opened the lid to find a tiny porcelain thimble designed to look like a hamburger fixed just the way she liked with mustard, ketchup, cheese, and pickle. "I guess I'm pretty much known for being a connoisseur of burgers!" Gingerly lifting it from the box, she displayed it on her index finger. "Leave it to you three to find a cheeseburger thimble! I love it!" She looked up at her collection. "Somewhere in heaven, Grandma is laughing up a storm!"

Annie put an arm around Mary Beth's shoulders. "We wanted to let you know we were thinking about you and wishing you were with us. You can find just about anything in New York City!"

Kate reached around her friends, pulled the paper bag off the counter, and handed it to Mary Beth. "And we brought you this because, well, it will be obvious when you see it."

Pulling a pale yellow T-shirt from the bag, Mary Beth shook it out and held it up to see the front. On it, a deliriously happy-looking woman with short gray hair was up to her elbows in different colors of yarn with "It's all about the yarn" embroidered above her.

Mary Beth pressed the shirt against her chest to check the size. "I think I resemble this woman!" She put the shirt on the counter. Grabbing the burger thimble, she immediately made a space in the center of the shadow box for her new addition to the collection. She looked at her friends and smiled. "Thank you for brightening my day. I really needed a lift."

Annie was just about to ask whether or not the Hook and Needle Club would meet the next morning when Stella's chauffeur, Jason, pushed open the door and held it as the regal, elderly woman entered the room slowly, albeit with grace.

"Well," Stella sniffed, taking in the obvious disarray of

the shop. "I came in to pick up some yarn, but I can hardly see how you can do business like this. I thought the cleanup would be further along by now."

Shrugging her shoulders, Mary Beth moved another box closer to the wall behind the register. "I hope to reopen in a couple of days."

Stella still looked a bit peaked, Annie thought. "How are you feeling?"

"I'm much better, although I will be glad when I am off all of the extra medication. The doctor is being overly cautious, but I guess that's why I pay him so much." Stella wrinkled her nose. "I'm still congested, but even I can smell the mildew in here. We simply cannot meet here tomorrow."

"That's true," said Mary Beth with a sigh. "I guess I've gotten used to the smell since I've been working in it for almost a week. I'm thankful the rain finally stopped. I suppose it wouldn't hurt us to miss a week."

"Nonsense," Stella replied. "We'll meet at my house. I'll have the housekeeper fix tea and scones. After all, we must be ready for the Polk family's fundraiser."

Annie was the first to find her voice after the shock of Stella's offer to open her home to the club. "Why, thank you, Stella, what a wonderful idea! That's very kind of you." Just when Annie thought she had Stella figured out, the prickly socialite showed a soft side.

"Yes," said Mary Beth, finally regaining her wits. "That means a lot to me. If Wally is here to oversee the repair work, maybe Kate and I can attend too. I'll call Peggy and Gwen about the change."

Stella smiled. "Then it's settled. I'll see everyone in my

parlor at eleven o'clock sharp!" With that, she silently took Jason's arm and walked out the door.

It had barely closed behind Stella when Alice erupted in laughter. "Well I'll be! In a week when we've been accosted once in a New York subway and had break-ins twice, doesn't this just take the cake? We're having tea in Stella's parlor!"

* * * *

Annie and Alice were still chuckling when they walked into The Cup & Saucer to pay Breck for taking care of Boots and to ask if he had noticed anything amiss at the house when he fed Boots on Sunday.

They were standing by the register, looking around the almost deserted diner, when Peggy walked up to them, her trusty pen and pad in hand. "Welcome home! How was New York City?"

"Very exciting. We have a lot to share at tomorrow's meeting," said Alice, peering through the window behind the counter to see if Breck was in the kitchen.

"You have your pick of tables today. It's been really slow." Peggy waved her hand as if this would magically fill the booths. "I'll be over to take your order in just a minute."

Annie took a couple of paces into the room and turned around. "Actually, we're just here to see Breck. Is he in today?"

"No, he was sent home early because business was so slow. You just missed him," Peggy explained. "Can I give him a message? He might return for the dinner hour."

Annie reached into her purse and pulled out an envelope with Breck's name on it. "Would you make sure he gets this?"

Peggy walked to the cash register and put the envelope under the cash drawer. "I'll keep it safe for him. See you at the meeting tomorrow!"

"Thank you." Annie started toward the door, but then she stopped and turned back to Peggy. "Oh, by the way, we just came from A Stitch in Time. Stella has offered to host tomorrow's meeting in her home. It's pretty noisy in the shop with all of the repair work going on. Stella said she would see us at eleven o'clock sharp."

Peggy's face fell. "I don't think I can get to Stella's house and back here in time for the lunch rush." She drummed her fingernails on the top of the register drawer. "I'll see if Lisa will swap shifts with me. Maybe I'll be able to make it."

"That's a good idea. I hope we'll see you tomorrow." Annie reached for the door again and led Alice through the doorway.

The three women said "Bye" in unison.

Alice and Annie walked out the door and headed to their next stop: the police station.

*   *   *   *

Pulling her car into the City Hall parking lot, Annie wondered if she'd run into Ian while in the building since the mayor's office was down the hall from police head-quarters. Ian was nowhere to be found, but Chief Edwards was sitting at his desk when the women walked into the station. He jumped to his feet as the door closed behind them. "Annie, Alice. How are you?"

"I'm well, but a bit tired after all of the excitement," Annie admitted.

Alice nodded in agreement. "I think we are both ready for some quiet time, believe it or not."

The chief riffled through his log book. "We kept patrolling Grey Gables throughout the night. When I saw your car at A Stitch in Time this morning, I sent Officer Peters to check the house. All was clear, but we didn't see any sign of the cat. Did it ever return?"

"No, she didn't," Annie said. "But on the positive side, neither did the intruder."

Chief Edwards looked back in his logbook. "We made regular patrols by Grey Gables while you were gone. Everything was fine when Cal drove by Saturday night. That leaves a narrow window when someone could have gotten in the house."

"Excuse me." Alice's hand stifled a yawn. "Neither of us got too much sleep last night. Annie here was up amazingly early to look for Boots. We searched the yard and the beach together after breakfast."

Chief Edwards walked to the fax machine and grabbed a stack of papers. Leafing through the sheets, he frowned. Obviously they weren't what he was expecting to find. "I'm still waiting for NYPD to fax me the report from your hotel room break-in. I did get in touch with Officer Fox, though. They don't have any leads right now. The perp didn't leave much behind in the way of fingerprints."

Annie kept glancing at the door, expecting Ian to walk in at any moment. She forced herself to concentrate on the conversation. "Will you let me know when you hear something from New York?"

Chief Edwards promised to call when he received any

new information. He also said Officer Peters would continue to assign extra patrols on her street for the next week or so. After promising to keep her doors and windows locked and to call if she saw anything out of the ordinary around the house, a disappointed Annie, who had hoped for some answers, left the station with Alice.

When the door closed behind them, Alice tapped Annie's arm. "You know, we can stick our head in the mayor's office and see if Ian is in."

The door to Ian's office was down the hall, and Annie looked longingly in its direction. Sometimes it seemed like Alice could read her mind. But was she ready to face Ian? "No, I really want to go home. I'll talk to Ian later."

*   *   *   *

Closing the door to Grey Gables, Annie felt the old house shudder as a faint echo filtered through its halls. The place seemed absolutely empty without Boots underfoot. Suddenly, Annie felt terribly alone. Tired and alone. Maybe she should have taken Alice up on her offer of lunch in the carriage house. But what if Boots returned, and she wasn't here?

Tossing her purse on the couch, she went upstairs to unpack her travel bag. She had been too tired and preoccupied to put everything away earlier. Then, in the morning, all she could think about was looking for Boots. She stared at her bed; the soft down comforter invited her to crawl in and take a nap. Annie was determined to get back to normal, and that meant unpacking—not napping.

When her toiletries had been returned to the bathroom and dirty clothes taken to the laundry area, she decided to work on the place mats so she'd have something to show the ladies at tomorrow's meeting.

Her keepsake from the trip to New York was a CD purchased at the club, *Live at The Avant-Garde*. She grabbed the disc, her cellphone, and the craft bag from her bedroom and carried them to the living room. Soon notes from Wynton Marsalis's trumpet filtered into the air as Annie curled up on the couch, crochet hook and yarn in hand. Losing herself in the music, her fingers worked swiftly until she heard loud rapping on the door.

After rolling her head around to clear the cobwebs, Annie went to the door. Ian swept her into a hug and held her in his arms for several moments before releasing her and cupping his hands around her face. "I just heard about the break-in here last night. Are you all right?"

She nodded, unable to speak. As he rubbed his thumbs along her jawline, he lowered his lips to hers in a kiss that left Annie with little doubt about his feelings. With closed eyes and pounding heart, she returned his kiss.

"I don't know what I would have done if anything had happened to you," he said, looking into her eyes.

Annie felt like he could see into her soul, which was probably good because words escaped her at the moment. She stepped away from him, and he followed her inside. She closed the door before taking his hand and leading him to the couch. She struggled to find her voice. "The police don't think we were ever in any danger, although nobody can figure out why things happened the way they did." She dared to glance into his eyes. They were filled with concern and care. "Thank you for checking on me."

Ian cleared his throat and took Annie's hands in his. "You know, when I called you at the hotel, I wanted to be there to make sure you really were safe. I wanted to be certain you wouldn't be in danger." He reached up and rubbed a lock of her hair between his fingers. "You've become so important to me, Annie."

Annie searched for the right words to say. She was unsure of how to define her feelings, much less explain them. "Ian, I care for you too." She struggled to keep her voice even. "I just need a little more time."

Silence enveloped them as they sat, fingers entwined, the CD having reached its end. They jumped a little when Annie's cellphone rang. She grabbed it before the second ring. "Hello?" A few seconds later, she rose and mouthed "NYPD" before strolling into the library and sitting at the desk. She pulled out a pad of scratch paper and a pen as Officer Fox asked her several more questions about the conference and how the women had spent their non-convention time in New York, which she answered as straightforwardly as possible. She jotted down the case number, plus the name and phone number of another officer also working the case. Officer Fox told her to call either of them if she remembered anything else about the trip. "I will. Thank you so much for calling," Annie said just before switching off the phone and returning to Ian, who was leafing through Charlie's book about New York City.

"That was Officer Fox from the New York Police Department. He didn't have any new information about the hotel break-in, but he asked some questions about the incident on the subway. I doubt if my answers helped too much."

Ian returned the book to the coffee table and stood up. "I wish he had called to say they had caught the burglar. Listen, Annie, if you need to return to New York to deal with any of this, I'd like to go with you."

She gave him a quick hug. "I doubt it will come to that. But thank you for the offer."

Ian glanced at his watch. "I need to get back to the office. I have a meeting in fifteen minutes. Be careful, please."

They walked to the door, and Annie followed him out to the porch. After he lightly kissed her again, she put her fingers to her lips and watched him walk to his car. When it disappeared down the driveway, Annie stepped from the porch and slowly moved her eyes from one end of the yard to the other. "Here, Boots! Here kitty, kitty!" Then she stood quietly for a long time, waiting to see some sort of movement in the brown grass. Seeing none, she rubbed her eyes and went into the house.

~ 18 ~

*P*iano music spilled into the foyer of Stella's mansion as Annie followed the housekeeper across the marble floor and past the conservatory, toward the parlor. Turning her head in the direction of the music, she found Jason sitting at a baby grand piano, his bobbing head bathed in the morning sunlight. Annie paused to watch as his hands glided over the keys.

Suddenly, as if unable to contain his voice any longer, he belted out the third verse, his face emanating pure joy. "Give my regards to Broadway, remember me to Herald Square, tell all the gang at Forty-Second Street that I will soon be there ..."

Annie stood mesmerized, clutching a craft tote in one hand and her purse in the other, until the doorbell rang. The housekeeper scampered back down the foyer to the front door. Before long, Gwen walked into the room with Peggy, Kate, and Mary Beth behind her.

"Look who I found in the driveway," said Gwen, shrugging out of her coat and handing it to the housekeeper.

The women whispered their greetings to one another, removed their coats, and joined Annie in watching the chauffeur's casual performance. When Jason sang the last note, they broke into applause. Pushing the piano bench back with a smile, he rose with a flourish and bowed. "Thank you! Just a little tune to mark the travelers' return from my hometown," he said. "May I escort you to the parlor?"

He stood just outside the open parlor door to allow the ladies to enter. "Mrs. Brickson will be with you momentarily. Please make yourselves comfortable," he said with a nod before leaving them.

The friends were just about to take their seats when Stella made her grand entrance, every piece of gray hair in her short "do" in place, a tailored pale blue dress falling in crisp folds around her calves. "Good morning, and welcome! I thought we'd have tea before getting started. There's coffee as well, for those who prefer it," she said, waving her friends over to the ornate Victorian chest opposite the fireplace.

The quintessential hostess stood at one end of the chest, inviting the ladies to a neat line of forks, folded napkins, and dainty cups and saucers. Glass plates were stacked next to a three-tiered silver tray offering levels of mini-quiches, sliced orange-glazed pound cake, and perfectly round scones. Small crystal bowls offered thick cream and what looked like boysenberry jam.

"Oh, Stella, this is lovely," said Gwen, pouring coffee from a silver pot into a cup. "Thank you for opening your home to us."

Stella nodded. "My pleasure. After all, we just couldn't have met in the shop. Between the odor and noise, we wouldn't have been able to hear ourselves think, much less conduct a conversation."

Mary Beth lifted a plate from the stack and moved toward

the food. "I must admit, this room is more conducive to crafting and conversation at the moment. I really appreciate your hosting this meeting, especially so soon after being ill."

"We all do," Annie added, carrying her plate and cup across the room to the sofa.

Soon the group was gathered in front of the fireplace, where tiny fingers of flames flickered between logs. When Stella was seated ramrod straight with her ankles crossed in one of the two leather chairs flanking the fireplace, silver forks began to clink against china plates.

Peggy placed her cup and saucer on the small accent table at the end of the couch, speared a bit of cake on her fork, and leaned her shoulder into Alice. "This is a great time to tell us about your trip," she said, popping the bite in her mouth.

Annie, Alice, and Kate took turns describing the conference, each reaching into her tote bag from time to time in search of materials gathered in workshops. They had collected enough copies of each brochure, handout, and sample to share with everyone.

Peggy organized hers into a pile on her lap before stuffing it into her craft bag. She looked at Annie, her eyes aglow with excitement. "This is great stuff! Now, let's hear about the jazz club."

"Well," Alice said, casting a dramatic look Peggy's way, "we found it our first night in the city. We learned the ins and outs of New York City subways and sidewalks, and found The Avant-Garde in Greenwich Village. We also met Mitchell Grants, the club's owner."

Stella looked puzzled. "The Avant-Garde? Why did you go there, exactly?"

"Oh, that's right!" Alice's confused look turned to one of understanding. "You were sick during the last meeting and didn't hear about Annie's latest mystery. She found an empty matchbook cover for a jazz club and some old photo negatives at Grey Gables. We were trying to trace the identity of a singer in one of them.

"Oh," said Stella stoically. "Carry on."

Annie, sitting on the other side of Alice, leaned forward on the couch. "Mr. Grants was a very nice man. He shared a lot of stories about the old days and some of my favorite jazz musicians."

Peggy crossed her legs and made circles in the air with her foot. "And? Did he know her?"

"Instantly. Her name was Asta, and she sang in the club during the late forties," Annie explained. Then she relayed the details Grants had provided.

The room was silent as Annie thought about what to say next. Suddenly Gwen said, "Stella?"

The older woman was pale and in obvious discomfort. "It's this cold and cough medicine that young doctor prescribed. It makes me lightheaded. I'm fine. Go on."

Alice whipped out her cellphone and began touching icons. "We found this photo of Asta in a café we visited with one of the club's musicians," she said, passing the phone around so each woman could see.

Stella barely glanced at the photo after taking the phone from Kate. Dropping it into her lap, she closed her eyes and leaned forward with her hands on her temples. "This medicine is getting to me."

Kate caught the phone with one hand as it slid from

Stella's lap and placed her other hand on the woman's shoulder. "Stella? Are you all right?"

Annie ran out of the parlor and called for Jason, who immediately appeared in the foyer. "I'm glad you're here," she said as he approached. "Stella isn't feeling well. Maybe she needs to lie down awhile."

He entered the parlor and went straight to his employer. Kneeling in front of her chair, he gently put a hand on her forearm. "Mrs. Brickson, can you stand? Would you like me to take you upstairs?"

Stella nodded, her expression blank. Standing slowly, she took Jason's arm.

Annie placed her hand on Stella's free arm. "Would you like me to help you upstairs?"

Stella stood up, grasping Annie and Jason for support, and started for the stairs. The rest of the Hook and Needle Club stayed in the parlor and watched the trio disappear.

Stella's gait seemed to improve as she moved closer to her bedroom. Color had nearly returned to her cheeks by the time Annie and Jason helped her get on the bed.

"Stella, I'm going to loosen the top few buttons on your dress to give you more breathing room, OK?" Annie waited for a nod before slipping the first button through its hole.

When Annie stood and stepped back from the bed, Jason took Stella's pulse and looked into her eyes. "Her pulse is fine," he said, turning to Annie. "Would you mind looking in the wardrobe and finding something less constricting for Mrs. Brickson to wear?"

Annie gave Jason a worried smile. "I'm happy to help."

Waving Jason's hand away, Stella cleared her throat as Annie turned toward the wardrobe. "I'm fine. I don't need to change clothes or go to bed."

Annie opened the mirrored door of the wardrobe and looked for a robe or loose housedress. When she found a velvety belted robe, Annie pushed back the next garment to make enough room to slip the cranberry material off the hanger.

"Annie, I'm fine! I don't need the robe." Stella's voice was suddenly strong and clear.

But Annie wasn't listening. She was too busy staring at Asta's countenance, her dark eyes flashing under a swoop of blond hair, gazing from a large, yellowed poster hanging in the back of the wardrobe. Pushing the clothes farther apart, Annie looked closer. It looked like the moody photo made from the negative found behind Gram and Grandpa's portrait but with the name "Asta" emblazoned in cursive across one top corner and the club's name and address printed along the bottom. Stunned, Annie struggled to make the connection between the cold, stubborn woman sitting on the nearby bed and the sultry songbird in the poster. Collecting her wits, she turned to Stella. "Asta. You knew Asta?"

Stella's eyes flashed, and then they narrowed. "Asta is none of your business!" Her voice was cold and razor sharp.

Jason looked from Annie to Stella and drummed his fingers on the dresser, drawing Annie's attention to the collection of family photos behind him. She crossed the room, her eyes searching each frame for familiar faces. Nestled in an antiqued silver frame, she found a black-and-white photo of a young Mitchell Grants posing with Asta in front of The Avant-Garde. "This is Mitchell Grants," Annie said, picking up the photo for a closer look. "I'd recognize his toothy smile anywhere."

Annie's eyes widened. She looked from Asta—smoldering, passionate, beautiful—to Stella—calm, cool, collected, and defiant. "Stella, are you Asta?"

Stella simply returned Annie's gaze without saying a word. Annie wondered if the woman was simply choosing her words carefully or refusing to answer the question altogether. While waiting for a reply, she perused the photos again and found a copy of the picture hanging in Marvin's Café, the same one Stella had been viewing when she dropped Alice's phone. Holding the photo closer, Annie studied the face of the man who was not Mitchell Grants. There was something about the eyes and the chin that reminded her of—Jason! She handed the photo to Jason. "Is this your father?"

Jason tapped his thumbs on the sides of the frame and looked to Stella with questioning eyes. His employer began to stammer an answer but then closed her mouth and nodded.

"This is my uncle, Leo Harmon. He was a photojournalist who died long before I was born." He replaced the photo in its original spot and selected another of Asta with a slightly older woman who looked to be in her mid-twenties. He tapped his index finger by her face. "My mother, Evelyn Harmon—Uncle Leo's sister. Before she married my father, she tagged along with my uncle on photo shoots. She was a gifted pianist who, I've been told, could keep up with the best jazz musicians at the time. She died in a car accident when I was a little boy."

Stella slowly rose from the bed and walked to the dresser. "Evelyn and I were good friends, just like Betsy and I were during our younger years. She was happiest when playing accompaniment for singers. Jason may look more like his Uncle Leo, but he inherited his mother's gift of music. He has made sure I keep music in my life."

Before Annie could respond, Alice's voice filtered in from the hallway. "Annie? Is everything all right?"

The room was silent for a moment as the three occupants looked at one another. Jason's eyes softened as he turned to Stella. "I think it is time to let your friends know Asta's identity and allow them to see a bit of the person you've hidden from them all this time."

Stella stammered as if trying to wrap her mind around the enormity of what Jason was asking her to do. Looking at Annie, she nodded. "Please tell our friends we will be down in a few minutes."

Stella sent Jason downstairs at the same time, assuring him she needed to be alone to collect her thoughts. Having done so, she descended the stairs on her own and entered the parlor.

"Thank you for waiting for me to weather the effects of my medication. I'm fine now. I've been out of commission with this cold and throat infection, so I didn't know about this latest mystery about Asta, the jazz singer," she said, her voice sounding much stronger than when she went upstairs. "Feel free to refill your cups and plates. You might want to have your works-in-progress handy to keep your hands occupied. Jason and I have quite the story to tell."

When all of the women had replenished their

refreshments and removed their needlework projects
from their bags, Stella took a deep breath and began to
tell her tale.

~ 19 ~

Stella stared at the marquee and could hardly believe her eyes. Oliver Franklin and His Band! They were really here, in New York City, opening at The Avant-Garde. It had been several years since they had played at the USO dance in Stony Point and had asked her to sing with them. She could still remember the curious mixture of nerves and excitement running through her body when she stepped up to the microphone and poured her heart out to the audience. Of course, she had nearly frozen when she spotted Betsy making eyes at Charlie Holden, but even losing the handsome sailor to Betsy couldn't take away the thrill of performing. All eyes had been on her during that song. There was nothing like it. Yet she never expected to see Oliver and the boys again.

"Just what's so special about this band, Stella, that you dragged us down here in the middle of the week?" Seymour Brickson asked.

Their friends Ruth and James were waiting by the club's entrance with Seymour's roommate, Clarence, and his girlfriend, Mildred.

Stella looked at Seymour and blinked. "I sang with them once at a USO dance a few years ago. They were good. Very good."

Taking her elbow, Seymour led her to their friends as people began arriving for the show. The six of them entered the club and found a table not too far from the stage. "I promise you will like this band," Stella said.

When Oliver and his band struck the first note, Stella closed her eyes and felt the music flow over her as she barely swayed her head to the music and tapped her toe, hidden under the table, firmly with each beat. They were still good. No wonder they hadn't faded away like many bands. She snapped out of her trance when Ruth touched her arm.

"Did you really sing with them? Onstage, in front of people?" Mildred cradled a highball glass between her hands.

Stella couldn't tell if Mildred's words indicated admiration or disgust. "Yes, I did," she replied. "All my years of music lessons culminated in that one performance at the USO dance." The truth of her reply fell softly, and Stella wondered why she had left music back in Stony Point with Betsy and Charlie. She looked at the past with the same hushed detachment as she had once watched snow flurries float from the sky into the yard of her childhood home. Being a singer against her father's wishes hadn't been any more possible than frolicking in the snow without his permission. Girls of her background just didn't do those things. The opportunity to perform had come and gone, replaced with her New York City debutante ball, sorority activities, and college classes.

At the end of the set, the band took a break and disappeared backstage. Mitchell Grants, the consummate club host, stopped by the table to see what everyone thought of the group. Much to the amusement of Stella's college friends, she told him about her one appearance with the band.

"Would you please ask Oliver if he will speak with me after the show? I'd enjoy seeing him after all these years," she said. "Tell him I am Stella from Stony Point, Maine."

Mitchell smiled, his pearly whites lighting up his face. "Will do. They will be back onstage shortly. Enjoy the rest of the show."

The band returned for the last set and drew loud applause after each number. Stella tried to divide her attention between the stage and the ongoing conversation at her table. She was only half-listening to Mildred describe a social event held recently at the Powelton Club when the music stopped and Oliver stepped to the microphone.

"Our final song goes out to a girl who jazzed up this band during a stop on our USO tour several years ago. This is *Stella by Starlight*."

Conversation at the table stopped as the band started to play. Stella was filled with a mixture of embarrassment and delight. She glanced at Seymour, who didn't seem to be amused by the bandleader's announcement. She remained silent after the song ended. Oliver stepped off the stage and made his way to Stella's table.

"Stella, it's good to see you after all these years," he said, pulling a chair from the next table and sitting down. "Are you still performing?"

Stella introduced Oliver to Seymour and their friends before answering. "No. I'm attending college in the city, but I've not had an opportunity to perform since I left Stony Point a few years ago. I'm flattered you remember me."

Oliver scraped his chair closer to Stella and looked into her eyes. "You were one of the best vocalists to perform with us on that tour. Say, we just lost our lead singer. Are you interested in auditioning?"

*   *   *   *

Stella's icy façade began to thaw, but the aristocratic bearing remained the same. As Stella began to weave the story, her eyes warmed, and Annie saw a glimpse of the passion so evident in the photographs of Asta performing.

"I suppose all of you are as scandalized as Seymour was when I told him about the audition." Stella looked into the faces of her friends, her hands folded in her lap.

How difficult this must be for Stella, Annie thought as she took in the surprised countenances of the Hook and Needle Club members, who had put down their projects and were focused solely on Asta's story.

"We're not scandalized," Annie said to fill the silence.

"It's more like we're surprised," finished Gwen, who then picked up her knitting needles and resumed work on a pink-and-purple cellphone case. "Quite surprised."

Kate shifted in her seat, her hands empty because she didn't have a work-in-progress to finish for the fundraiser. "Mr. Grants said Leo Harmon was in love with Asta, or I guess I mean he was in love with you. What happened between the two of you?"

Stella's response was a smile bigger than Annie had ever seen on her grandmother's childhood friend.

"Leo is how I found Jason. He was Jason's uncle," Stella said, looking at her chauffeur. "But I am getting ahead of myself."

Little by little, Stella unraveled the mystery of the jazz singer and the photos found at Grey Gables. Oliver Franklin and His Band—featuring Asta—became a hit in New York and drew crowds at each performance. One of their biggest fans was a photojournalist named Leo Harmon.

"Leo was a kind, shy man who hid behind his camera. He loved photography, jazz music, and Asta. He often dropped by the club to take photos of musicians during rehearsals or performances. When he couldn't afford to pay to see the show, he happily exchanged photos for a ticket."

She fell silent as if deciding which memories to share and which to keep locked away in the past.

"He was filled with stories about jazz musicians he had met through his photography, and he delighted in telling those tales, especially to me," Stella said. "I was a young, small-town girl with stars in her eyes. I thought I could have it all, money, status, and music. I was naive."

Annie's eyes skipped from face to face, and she wondered what her friends were thinking. She watched Kate shift again in her chair.

"Stella, did you love Leo?" asked Kate, her question barely audible.

Annie was curious to hear the answer and laid her partially made place mat and crochet hook across her thighs in anticipation of the answer.

"Kate, Leo was in love with a woman who really didn't exist. Asta wasn't real. She was just a figment of a young girl's imagination, a girl who mistakenly believed she could keep her left foot in one world and her right foot in another."

Stella hesitated and seemed to be at a loss for words. An awkward silence hung over the room.

Jason, who had pulled up a chair between Stella and the fireplace, cleared his throat. "Pardon me for interrupting, but this might be a good time to tell them about my mother."

Stella nodded and asked Jason to pour her a glass of water. She watched as he crossed the room to the refreshments and filled a tall glass from a china pitcher. "Thank you," she said before taking a sip and continuing her story.

"Evelyn." The name was spoken with awe and affection Annie hadn't before heard from Stella. "Leo's sister was one of the most talented pianists I've ever known. Ten years Leo's junior, she was in awe of her brother and his friendships with musicians. She didn't like to perform alone, but she loved to accompany anyone who happened to be playing at the club."

Stella and Evelyn had been close friends, drawn together by a love of music and the realization that neither one of them would ever become famous—Stella by virtue of her limiting social status and Evelyn because of a debilitating fear of performing before large crowds.

"We came from different worlds, Evelyn and I, but we shared a great love for music. Isn't it interesting how music can bridge the gap between people? If it hadn't been for jazz, we never would have met, much less become friends," Stella said. "In many ways, she was like Betsy, very accepting of people and their faults." Stella's eyes fell on Annie. "Evelyn became the confidant I lost when I cut your grandmother out of my life. She was the only person I trusted enough to share why I had left Stony Point. Nobody else knew my heart was broken when Charlie Holden fell in love with Betsy instead of me. Jealousy can make a person do such stupid things! For a time, Leo and Evelyn were like the brother and sister I never had."

Annie and Alice exchanged glances. *We understand the importance of Stella's words,* Annie thought. Alice had been like a sister to Annie during those summers she spent in Stony Point as a child. They immediately reestablished that bond when Annie returned. Stella and Betsy never had that chance.

"Mind you," Stella continued, "Leo also very nearly ruined my life."

～ 20 ～

Asta stepped into the spotlight and wrapped her gloved hands around the microphone as piano music filled the smoky air. Conversation in the club stopped as she took a deep breath and released a soft, low note and built it to a crescendo before launching into a sultry version of Billie Holiday's *I Love My Man*.

Music worked its magic, and the small-town girl who grew up with wealth and privilege sang emotionally of loving a man who treated her badly. She felt the power of the song and the adoration of the crowd, first harnessing, then releasing them in her voice. The audience was mesmerized, and Asta knew it. She loved the power in performing, her true identity hidden behind the blond wig and the old Scandinavian form of her name. As Asta, she became the women in her songs with life experiences that Stella would never know.

Her concentration was broken by a sudden flash of light from in front of the stage. She looked down to see a tall, dark-haired man adjusting settings on a heavy-looking camera. It was Leo Harmon, the photographer from the newspaper and a semipermanent fixture at the club. Why did he show up now? Her composure regained, Asta had no choice but to carry on and ignore the camera. But the more photos he took, the tighter fear gripped her. How would Seymour react if a photo of her turned up in print?

The song over, Asta disappeared offstage as the band transitioned into an original instrumental number. She ducked into her dressing room to compose herself. *What's the worst that can happen?* she thought. The photos might be published in the paper, but would people recognize the blond, sultry singer as willowy, dark-haired Stella? She checked her wig and lipstick in the mirror and studied her reflection. Seymour would know it was her, and it could jeopardize their future. He'd never forgive her if she brought embarrassment on his family. She must stop Leo from using her photograph!

The band reached the end of their song, and Asta hurried to the stage to sing her final two numbers. Having decided how to handle the photo situation, she gave herself completely to the music.

At the end of the set, Leo spent time taking shots of instruments, sheet music, and whatever personal items he could round up from the musicians—a glass of ice cubes left onstage by Oliver, a felt hat belonging to the trumpet player. Asta had found her opportunity to speak to him alone.

"Leo, I need your help," she pleaded, grabbing his shirtsleeve. She knew Evelyn's brother had feelings for her, and that gave her an advantage. "I need you to destroy the photos you took of me tonight. I'll pay you for them, but please get rid of the film."

Asta knew Evelyn had told Leo about Seymour and his displeasure about her singing. Leo would understand. He put his cumbersome camera on the top of the upright piano and turned back to Asta.

"I'm here on official business for the newspaper, so I can't sell you the photos," he said, looking into her eyes with a tenderness Stella had not yet experienced from Seymour. "But I'll dispose of the film containing shots of you. As far as anyone knows, we never had this conversation."

*   *   *   *

Stella unclasped her hands and placed them on the arms of the chair. "We never spoke of it again. I thought he had destroyed the photos because when the piece about the club was published in the paper, my photo wasn't included," she said. "The singer Asta was briefly mentioned in the accompanying story, but the name Stella was never associated with her. Leo and Evelyn kept my secret for the rest of their lives."

Peggy pulled a stitch through the finished edge of her quilt and looked up at Stella. "What happened to them?" Movement stopped in the room and all eyes fell on Stella.

"Leo took a job as a war correspondent and was sent to Korea. I never saw him again," Stella said. "Evelyn and I grew up and faced reality. We each married. I became Mrs. Seymour Brickson, which carried certain social responsibilities, and she had a baby. When Asta disappeared from my life, in a sense, so did Evelyn."

The two women, separated by social class, had kept in touch occasionally through Christmas cards. From time to time, Evelyn had sent photos of Jason—coming home from the hospital as an infant, sitting on his mother's lap at the piano, dressed for his first day of school.

"He showed great talent for the piano at a young age," Stella said, looking at Jason. "Evelyn was very proud of that.

She taught him herself, and later she found a way to pay for his piano lessons."

Jason looked embarrassed to be the center of the discussion. "When Mom was killed, Mrs. Brickson arranged for me to continue my piano lessons. After I graduated from high school, my father couldn't afford to send me to college, and Mrs. Brickson offered me a job. I've been with her ever since."

Peggy, who had grown up wanting to be a teacher but put college on hold to marry and have a family, seemed particularly moved by Stella's story.

"Do you miss it? Performing, I mean."

Stella seemed lost in thought for a moment. "Eventually I had to choose between Seymour and jazz. While jazz was my passion, sensibility opted for marriage." She looked at each woman in the room. "Did I make the right choice? I made the only choice that I thought I could. Seymour and I had a good marriage based on friendship—friendship that grew into love. I truly grieved when he died," she said, "but never again did anything make me feel quite like I did when Asta was onstage at the greatest jazz club in New York."

Kate, obviously still basking in the afterglow of the flirtation with Cole, leaned closer to Stella. "You said Leo didn't really know you. But maybe he really did know—and love you—even though he met you as Asta instead of Stella. After all these years, he sort of reached out from another world to remind this world that Asta really had existed."

Just when Annie thought Stella was starting to wilt, Alice created a diversion.

"There must be something magical about that club, some sort of airborne love dust," Alice said, her eyes dancing, "because Kate experienced a jazzy spark in New York City too."

Suddenly all eyes in the room shifted from Stella to Kate, who squirmed in her chair. "Alice! This isn't about me."

Mary Beth's jaw dropped. "You were at the shop all day yesterday, and you didn't mention a thing! I guess I should have known something was up when you kept checking your phone for text messages! That just isn't like you, unless Vanessa is away from home."

Gwen, less given to gossip than Mary Beth, cast a sympathetic smile in Kate's direction. "Kate, naturally we want to hear your news, but only when you are ready to tell it," she said, flashing an unspoken warning to the others.

Once Kate recovered from the embarrassment of Alice's sudden declaration—and after her cheeks returned to their normal color—she began to fill in the details surrounding Alice's impromptu announcement. "His name is Cole Cutchins, and he is a trumpet player," she explained. "I bumped into him and spilled his drink during his band's break during our first visit to The Avant-Garde. But he was so nice about it that we ended up talking the entire intermission."

Alice couldn't contain herself any longer. "And he was cute too!"

Kate giggled. "Yes, he was cute too. We saw him three different times. He even took us to dinner at his favorite café, which is where Alice found Asta's photo on the wall."

Noticing a Mona Lisa smile on Stella's face, Kate stopped, paused, and realized Jason was nodding his head as if this was old news. "What is it?" she asked.

Getting a nod from Stella, Jason replied, "We heard."

Everyone except Stella began talking at once, demanding to know how the news had reached Jason first. When the buzz among the women died down, Jason continued. "The jazz world is very connected—everyone seems to know each other one way or another."

Annie sat quietly, trying to follow the story as it became more complicated. She hoped Jason would tie together all of the loose ends soon. Jason explained how Ernst Michaels, a fan of both jazz music and the work of Leo Harmon, had tracked him down years earlier while working on a research project on the history of the New York jazz scene with a newspaper correspondent. Mr. Michaels kept him up to date on the music world.

"Ernst knew I was Leo Harmon's nephew, but he wasn't aware that I worked for the woman he knew as the jazz singer named Asta. Remember, she resumed using her real name when she married Mr. Brickson," Jason said.

As prickly as Stella could be, Annie had always noticed uncharacteristic warmth in her voice when she spoke to the chauffeur. A real affection seemed to flow between them despite their formal way of addressing each other. Like his uncle, Jason had kept Stella's secret, another sign of his high regard for her.

Jason slowly tied each string of the mystery together, each strand leading back to The Avant-Garde. Cole Cutchins, he said, first met Ernst Michaels because of the photojournalist's frequent visits to the club. Later, Cutchins helped Michaels compile a book about contemporary jazz musicians in New York City jazz clubs.

"Ernst could hardly contain himself when he pulled the

prints of Uncle Leo's negatives out of the developing solution. He recognized them as my uncle's work immediately and called to tell me of your discovery." Jason grinned impishly and looked at Alice. "He also said the redhead was a real looker."

Mary Beth burst out laughing. "Alice, that's New York speak for saying you are hot!"

Tossing her hair, Alice imitated a fashion model pose. "That's me. I'm a looker!"

When the laughing subsided, Jason explained the significance of Annie's discovery. Leo had been an accomplished photographer in his time, but he was still a young man in his early thirties when he died. He stored many of his old photos and negatives at his parents' house in Ohio when he left for Korea, but his jazz works weren't among them. When the music experienced a renewed popularity in the 1980s, experts began asking about Leo Harmon's lost jazz negatives.

"Who would have guessed they'd turn up in an attic in Maine sixty years after he was killed while on assignment in Korea?" Jason said.

"I sure didn't." Stella said. "And I didn't expect to see my photo on Alice's cellphone!"

"That much was pretty obvious," Alice said, laughing. "But how did you know we had been to The Avant-Garde?"

Jason resumed his tale.

Shortly after Annie, Alice, and Kate had left the club, Cole Cutchins called Ernst with the news that three women from Stony Point, Maine, had showed up at The Avant-Garde with photos printed from Leo Harmon negatives. He turned to Kate. "Ernst also asked me if I knew you. He said Cole had fallen hard and fast for the quiet Kate. Each time Cole called Ernst with an update on Kate and your quest to determine Asta's identity, he kept me posted on your activities."

Annie closed her eyes and tried to absorb the details of Jason's story. She was still a bit confused when she opened them. "When did you tell Stella about our trip to The Avant-Garde?"

Annie detected a bit of guilt on Jason's face.

"I told her about your trips to The Avant-Garde and Cole's infatuation with Kate after your first trip to the club. But I didn't want to upset her with news of your questions about Asta." He turned to Stella. "I'm sorry I didn't tell you about the photos. I figured the issue would go away since your friends didn't find out any concrete evidence of Asta's true identity. I should have known the mystery would be a group project."

Annie realized Jason had been protecting Stella from her past. "A lot of strange things have happened—the phone call, the threatening man on the subway, the ransacked hotel room, and the intruder at Grey Gables. Who was responsible for those?"

Jason's eyes widened as he shook his head. "I have no idea. Ernst only told me about the photos and your arrival at the club. And he asked questions about Kate for Cole. Were any of you hurt? Was anything stolen?"

Annie's eyes filled with tears. "Boots is gone. I've not seen her since last Thursday morning. The door to Grey Gables was open when we came home, and Boots was no-where to be found."

Pulling a tissue from her bag, Annie dabbed her eyes.

Her eyes burned, and fatigue had caught up with her. She wasn't the only one who was overwhelmed. Though every bit as prim and proper as she had been when the group arrived, Stella seemed tired after her trek into the past. It was time for them to go.

"Thank you, Stella, for hosting our meeting and trusting us with your story," Annie said, giving a meaningful look to her friends. "Unless you want to share it with others, your secret identity will be held in confidence."

Stella looked relieved, although Annie wasn't sure if it was because her secret was finally out or because the meeting was coming to an end. A chorus of "thank you" was added by the other women as they gathered their belongings.

The ladies dispersed, and Annie was soon speeding home in her trusty Malibu. She was still trying to wrap her mind around Stella and Asta being the same person, a yin and yang inside one person. The mystery of the jazz singer was solved, even though she still had no idea how Leo Harmon's negatives landed in her attic.

She turned into the driveway leading to Grey Gables, thinking of Jason's reaction to the break-in and the disappearance of Boots. Although he had been protecting Stella from her past, Jason had seemed genuinely surprised when Annie had mentioned the phone call during the convention as well as the subway incident. Surely he didn't have anything to do with the incidents.

Annie parked the car and spent some time walking around the yard and calling for Boots. She took the path through the windy dunes to the beach and doubled back to circle the house, stopping from time to time to call the cat's name. Her heart heavy, Annie trudged up the steps to the porch. Plopping down in a wicker chair, Annie leaned her head back and closed her eyes. "Boots, where are you?"

~ 21 ~

Leo sat cross-legged in the sand and watched Charlie's daughter, Judy, toddle to the sea and giggle as the water washed over her feet. The water ebbed and flowed, and in a particularly strong rush, knocked the little girl off her feet. He grabbed his camera as she reacted to the spill by throwing fistfuls of water and sand into the air with sheer abandonment. "Lele! Lele!" she cried with joy when she spied her father's war buddy creeping through the sand, his camera poised in the air. He responded by taking shot after shot of the gleeful girl, whose pink-and-yellow swimsuit was now covered with wet sand.

His photographic instincts taking over, Leo suddenly pivoted in the sand, and dropping to one knee, quickly snapped several frames of Charlie and Betsy looking at their daughter, their eyes sparkling with adoration. *This*, he thought, *is as good as it gets.* The late afternoon sun cast a golden glow across the beach—providing the best light for capturing the delight of a small child and the obvious love of her parents.

Leo placed his camera on a towel and ran toward little Judy. Grabbing her waist, he swept her high over his head and reveled in her giggles. His heart swelled with love for this family. Coming here to visit Charlie before heading to Korea had been the right thing to do. He was heading off to document the devastation of war, armed with memories of fishing with Charlie and little Judy, savoring Betsy's rhubarb pie, and swapping war stories with the man who had saved his life in the Pacific. That was when he had acquired the nickname "Shooter," a nickname that would follow him into his career as a professional photographer. He knew these were moments he'd recall over and over again while covering the war in Korea for the newspaper. Yes, he was headed back into a war zone, but this time his weapons would be a pen and camera instead of firearms. He'd need good memories to temper the visions of death he knew would surround him on the battlefield.

After a hearty meal and a card game with Charlie and Betsy, Leo climbed the stairs to the guest room. Later, when he heard his friends close the door to their bedroom, he gathered several bottles, a bundle of paper, a few odds and ends, and the film from his camera before slipping down the hall to the bathroom. He surveyed his work space—he'd worked in worse conditions. By the end of the week, when he was scheduled to return to New York before heading to Korea, a nice set of family portraits would be ready to give his friends as a remembrance of the visit.

Friday arrived all too soon, and Leo packed his bag with reluctance. The days at Grey Gables had been idyllic. He gathered the portraits—one of Betsy and Charlie, and the other with the couple holding little Judy—and negatives from the film he shot during his visit.

He walked to the window and gazed at the ocean, wondering if he'd ever see Charlie again. His friend had helped him cheat death once; could he escape it again? Would they have another chance to listen to jazz at The Avant-Garde and debate whether Stan Getz or Charlie Parker was the best saxophone player in the world?

Since visiting his parents in Ohio, Leo had wondered what to do with the photo negatives from his photo shoots at the club. He had carried them from New York to Ohio and now to Maine. Where would they be safe? The answer was clear now—they belonged here with Charlie. The man who saved his life would keep them until they could listen to music together again.

He pulled the tin containing the negatives from his duffle bag, removed the lid, and sifted through the strips, stopping occasionally to hold one up to the window. Smiling, he singled out a particular strip and stared at it a long time, remembering the sultry Asta who had turned out to be Betsy's childhood friend from Stony Point. Despite his promise to her, he hadn't been able to bring himself to destroy the negatives. He'd kept thinking she'd someday want to remember her time of performing jazz at The Avant-Garde in New York City.

He slipped the negatives of Asta in with those of the portraits. Hefting his duffle with one hand and slinging it over his shoulder, he grasped the portraits and tin containing the jazz photo negatives in the other and headed downstairs to say goodbye.

* * * *

Annie woke with a disoriented start when she felt a brush against her leg. Realizing she was still outside, Annie looked down, one arm poised to swat the offending critter, and found a wide-eyed Boots staring back at her. "Boots!" she cried, scooping the cat into her arms and burying her face in her fur. "Do you have any idea how much I love you?" Tears welled in Annie's eyes, and she allowed them to flow down her cheeks, laughing at the cat's curious expression. It felt great to cuddle the impish feline in her arms again. "I've been so worried about you!"

Annie reveled in the feel of the gray fur beneath her fingers, the soothing sound of the cat's loud, satisfying purr, and the light tickle as her fuzzy tail curled around her wrist.

She closed her eyes in heartfelt gratitude. "Thank you, God, for bringing Boots back home to Grey Gables and to me," she said, scratching the cat behind her ears. Looking into the green eyes, Annie realized just how much love she'd found here in Stony Point. *A person has to be careful when it comes to love,* she thought. *Love is something hard to come by and easy to lose.*

"I love you, Boots, and I almost lost you," Annie whispered in the cat's ear. "Whatever would I have done without you?"

Suddenly her mind was clear, the confusion and haze lifted, leaving behind a sense of acute clarity. Was her reluctance to define her feelings putting her in danger losing Ian too? Her heart, she realized, was big enough to hold the memory of Wayne, the love for her family, and allow room for Ian also.

"Oh, Boots!" she exclaimed. "I love Ian too!" She had never uttered those words—not even to Alice. She looked down at her furry confidant. "That really is OK, isn't it?"

It seemed like the cat was looking right through

Annie's eyes and into her soul. "Meow!" And with that, Boots jumped off Annie's lap and stood at the door, waiting for her to open it.

*   *   *   *

The day of the Polk family fundraiser had arrived, but Annie had a personal task to take care of before she could leave for the community center.

She carried the two heavy wooden portrait frames from the library window seat to the desk. Her intention to replace the old photographs with restored copies had been forgotten during the recent excitement—the trip to New York City, Boots's disappearance, and Stella's revelation about Asta. Annie felt the need to get it done. She turned the frames over so the backs were facing up. Holding the first of two paper sleeves open with one hand, she gingerly pulled the portrait out and placed it on the desk.

The vivid images of Betsy and Charlie startled her. Details long ago faded from the original photograph had reappeared in the copies Ernst Michaels had made from the negative. Charlie's hair was darker; Betsy's was lighter. The collar of her dress, difficult to see in the original portrait, was more defined and clearly made of delicate crocheted lace. Annie's eyes moved up the photograph. What had looked like a studio wall in the faded originals was really a horizon. She bent closer and examined the space were the land met sky. *There's Butler's Lighthouse!* She let this thought sink in until she realized the significance of Stony Point's most recognizable landmark standing in the background of the photo. Leo Harmon had spent time here at Grey Gables.

Annie placed the restored photo in the frame and slid the matching negatives in the pocket where they had been found. Then she did the same thing to the family portrait featuring cherubic Judy with a hand stretched out as if greeting the photographer. It must have been taken in the same spot as the other portrait, because the lighthouse stood faintly in the distance. They looked so happy, as if they were posing for a keepsake photo to remember a special day.

One at a time, she returned each portrait to its original place on the library wall. Stepping back, she looked at the smiling faces and felt the joy emanating from them. Leo had certainly caught their loving spirit. She remembered the photos of Charlie taken while visiting historical places in New York City. They bore the initials L.H. Leo must have taken those too. Stella's story of Asta ran through her mind, and Annie remembered how Leo had kept his promise not to publish photos of the singer. He cared about Asta so much that he had found a way to keep the negatives safe in case she ever wanted to have photos as a memento of her time as a jazz singer.

Annie was lost in her reverie until Boots began making figure eights around her legs. She scooped the cat into her arms and rubbed her cheek on her fuzzy gray head before looking at the wall clock. "Are you reminding me it's time to head to the community center?" The cat's only response was a loud purring as Annie put on her coat and grabbed the rhubarb pie she had baked before heading out the front door.

*　*　*　*

The smell of hamburgers frying and popcorn popping filled the community center as the six-member high school vocal ensemble assembled onstage and belted out a medley of Carrie Underwood hits. Annie and Reverend Wallace strolled among the rows of booths as she waited her turn to work the Hook and Needle Club table.

"How are you, Annie?" Reverend Wallace asked, his voice tinged with concern.

Annie stopped walking as a group of young teenagers scampered by to peruse the bake sale table. "My emotions seem to ebb and flow, but right now I feel calm and at peace. It's definitely been a soul-searching time. Losing Boots for a while certainly put things in perspective."

The pastor took Annie's hand in his. "Your face looks quite serene—radiant even. This is a big change since I last saw you. Just remember, I am here if you need to talk. Please don't hesitate to call me."

Annie squeezed his hand. "I will, Reverend Wallace, I promise."

Just as the minister walked away to check on members of the Polk family, who were scheduled to take the stage later in the morning, Annie heard her name called from across the room and saw Breck hurrying toward her. When he came to a stop, he dug a key and a wad of greenbacks from his front pocket and handed them to her.

Breck looked at the floor. "Thank you for dropping the money by the diner, but I don't feel right taking it after losing your cat."

Annie's eyes widened. "You did what?"

A contrite Breck explained how he was late leaving the diner on Saturday, and Boots was waiting by the door when he arrived. The cat dashed out of the house and disappeared before he could catch her.

"I chased her and looked all over, but I couldn't find her in the dark," Breck explained, hanging his head. "I was too embarrassed to tell you, 'specially after Peggy told everyone at the diner about the break-in and the missing cat. I was scared too. With my background, I was afraid someone might think I was involved in a break-in. I'm really sorry, Mrs. Dawson."

Annie gave Breck an impulsive hug. "Boots came home. She's fine! I'm thankful she is safe, and it's a relief to know there really wasn't a break-in at Grey Gables after all! I'll let Chief Edwards know he can close the case."

She could tell the teen felt badly about what had happened. He probably hadn't closed the door all the way, although he had locked it, in his haste to find the runaway cat. The wind must have blown it open. Breck had been so preoccupied with finding Boots that he didn't go back to check the door.

"Please don't worry about letting Boots out of the house. The lock is tricky, and Boots can be pretty slippery sometimes!" Annie said.

She looked at the wad of bills in her hand and flattened them between her palms. "You did a good job, Breck. The lock on the front door of Grey Gables sticks. It's happened to me too. I want you to keep this." She held the money out to him.

The teen looked a little surprised and embarrassed, but his lips curled in a slight smile. He reached out and slowly pulled the bills from her fingers. "Thank you." He stuffed the money into his pocket. "I'm really glad the cat is OK. I, uh, I really need to get back."

Annie watched Breck lope across the community center to resume his post with Peggy at the diner's booth. He'd come a long way since first starting work at The Cup & Saucer. While still a bit rough around the edges, the surliness was gone. People were beginning to see beyond the long, wavy hair and baggy clothes to realize there was a smart, caring young man hiding there.

The soft notes of a trumpet lifted into the air from the stage and built into an intricate crescendo before dropping back into a soft melody. Annie felt Ian's presence beside her before she heard him speak her name. "Ian!" she exclaimed, with heartfelt enthusiasm. "Good morning!"

He dropped a quick kiss on her cheek. "Who's the trumpet player? He's good."

Annie nodded and looked to the Hook and Needle Club table where Kate stood beaming beside Alice and Gwen. "That's Cole Cutchins, the musician we met in New York at The Avant-Garde."

Ian raised his eyebrows. "Impressive. How did Vanessa get him to play here?"

"A little Kate magic," Annie said to the confused mayor. "Kate and Cole really bonded at the club and remained in touch after we returned to Stony Point. When Cole heard about little Matthew Polk's surgery, he wanted to help."

"Well, he certainly adds something to the festivities."

Ian tapped his fingers to the beat on the coffee cup he was holding. "It was nice of him to take the time to support our community event. Will you introduce us later?"

"Absolutely," said Annie, taking his arm and steering him toward the needlecraft table. "I need to check in and see if I'm needed to man the booth yet. Walk with me?"

Ian nodded. "Just don't let me forget to pick up the rhubarb pie they are holding for me at the bake sale."

"I think I can remember that!" she said. "Can you eat an entire pie?"

He patted his trim waist. "Oh, I don't think that will be a problem."

They strolled arm in arm across the room. Gazing at the table, Annie was surprised to see only two of her place mat and coaster sets on display. "Maybe we should put out more of my items."

Gwen moved the two sets to the center of the table. "I would—if there were any more left. I predict these two will be gone before noon."

Alice lifted her eyes and hands from the cash box sitting in front of her. "We've made $325 so far!"

Annie watched the people of Stony Point meander around the community center in search of purchases to help support the Polks. She looked at Kate, who was studying every nuance of Cole's performance as if trying to burn it into her memory. Ian's arm now rested lightly across Annie's shoulders, and she leaned in a bit closer. Love, or something very close to it, was definitely in the air.

A little before noon, Stella arrived early to take her shift at the booth. But first she motioned for Annie to follow her

into the hallway outside the community room. Annie, curious to find out why she was being summoned to the hall,
excused herself and told Ian she'd catch up to him later.

The hallway was quiet after the two women closed the
door behind them. "Stella, is everything all right?"

"Yes," Stella replied. "I just have something to tell you,
and I didn't want to do it in front of the entire town." Her
face softened. "I'm afraid actions I took as an impetuous
young woman recently caused you unnecessary angst. You
see, Mitchell Grants phoned to say he was still making good
on his decades-old promise to keep my past a secret."

Mitchell, it turned out, had hired the man who had
threatened Annie, Alice, and Kate on the subway in an attempt to prevent them from returning to the club and discovering Asta's true identity. He was also the one who had
left the fake message for Kate and had ransacked their
hotel room.

"Strangely, Mitchell said he didn't know a thing about
the intruder who broke into Grey Gables," Stella said.

"Oh, it turned out there wasn't an intruder after all,"
Annie said, relating Breck's apology for letting Boots out of
the house. "All is well. No harm, no foul."

Stella was unblinking. "Annie, I hope that means you
don't intend to press charges. Mitchell was simply trying to
protect an old friend. He didn't mean any harm."

Annie thought of the elderly man who was so gracious
with his time. "He was very good to us. I admire anyone so
dedicated to keeping a promise. I can't speak for Alice and
Kate, but I don't see any reason to press charges."

Annie opened the door to the community center for

Stella. "Thank you for telling me about Mr. Grants. I can't say I wasn't unnerved by his actions, but it means a lot when someone keeps his word—especially for sixty years!"

"Indeed," Stella said, and she walked through the doorway.

Stella and Annie, who were relieving Alice and Gwen of their duties, walked together to the Hook and Needle Club table where Vanessa was waiting with an update on the fundraiser.

"Between the bake sale, barbecue lunch, car wash, and rummage sale, the student council has raised over $5,000 for the family so far," Vanessa said, "and we still have a couple of hours left!"

Kate rearranged the merchandise on the club's table. "And don't forget that Cole plans to donate everything from his tip jar to the Polks too."

As if he had heard his name, Cole cleared his throat and spoke into the microphone on the stage. "This next song was inspired by and is dedicated to my new friend Kate, who led me to this charming town of Stony Point, and to the beautifully mysterious jazz singer, Asta, who brought us all together."

Kate's face turned a rosy pink, but her smile was even brighter.

Alice stood next to Annie, her purse draped on her shoulder in preparation for making her contribution to the fundraising effort with a few purchases. "Oh Kate, now you are a celebrity!"

"Yes," said Gwen, half in teasing and half with admiration. "Not everyone is lucky enough to be publicly serenaded by a handsome man, with a song he wrote for her, no less!"

Stella, sitting at the club's table away from the group, smiled with a slight twinkle in her eye. Annie and Ian stood together, perched on the edge of something new in their relationship. As they exchanged a smile, Annie slipped her hand in his and squeezed.

Kate's laugh filtered between them. "It is pretty cool to have a man memorialize me in a song. But don't make it into more than it really is," she said. "We have a mutual understanding—he doesn't intend to leave New York City, and I don't plan on moving away from Stony Point."

This, Annie thought, *is the perfect day.* She watched Cole play for a moment before glancing at Stella. She had returned to the embracing arms of Stony Point, to the same folks who adopted Mary Beth when she fled the city and the boyfriend who had dumped her years ago. Here, in the community center of this tiny town, one-time strangers were giving their time, money, and talents to help the Polk family make it through a difficult situation. Annie knew firsthand that it took time to build trust and friendships in this close-knit town. But once those ties were bound, they stayed that way.

The Polk family—Mac and Tinia and all four children—laughed and hugged their way around the room, thanking friends and neighbors for helping them pay for little Matthew's eye surgery. Their plan, like those before them, was to pay it forward and contribute to the next community event held to help others needing a hand.

Annie was aware that the once-overwhelming tug to

return to Texas was becoming fainter as time passed. She would always have LeeAnn, Herb, and the twins back there, but Grey Gables, Boots, and a new family of treasured friends now kept her anchored in this town with a history integrally entwined with her own. Annie draped an arm around Kate's shoulder as they watched the trumpeter point the bell of his horn to the ceiling and belt out a high note.

"Oh, I don't know if Cole will be able to resist Stony Point," Annie said to Kate. "This place sort of gets in your blood."